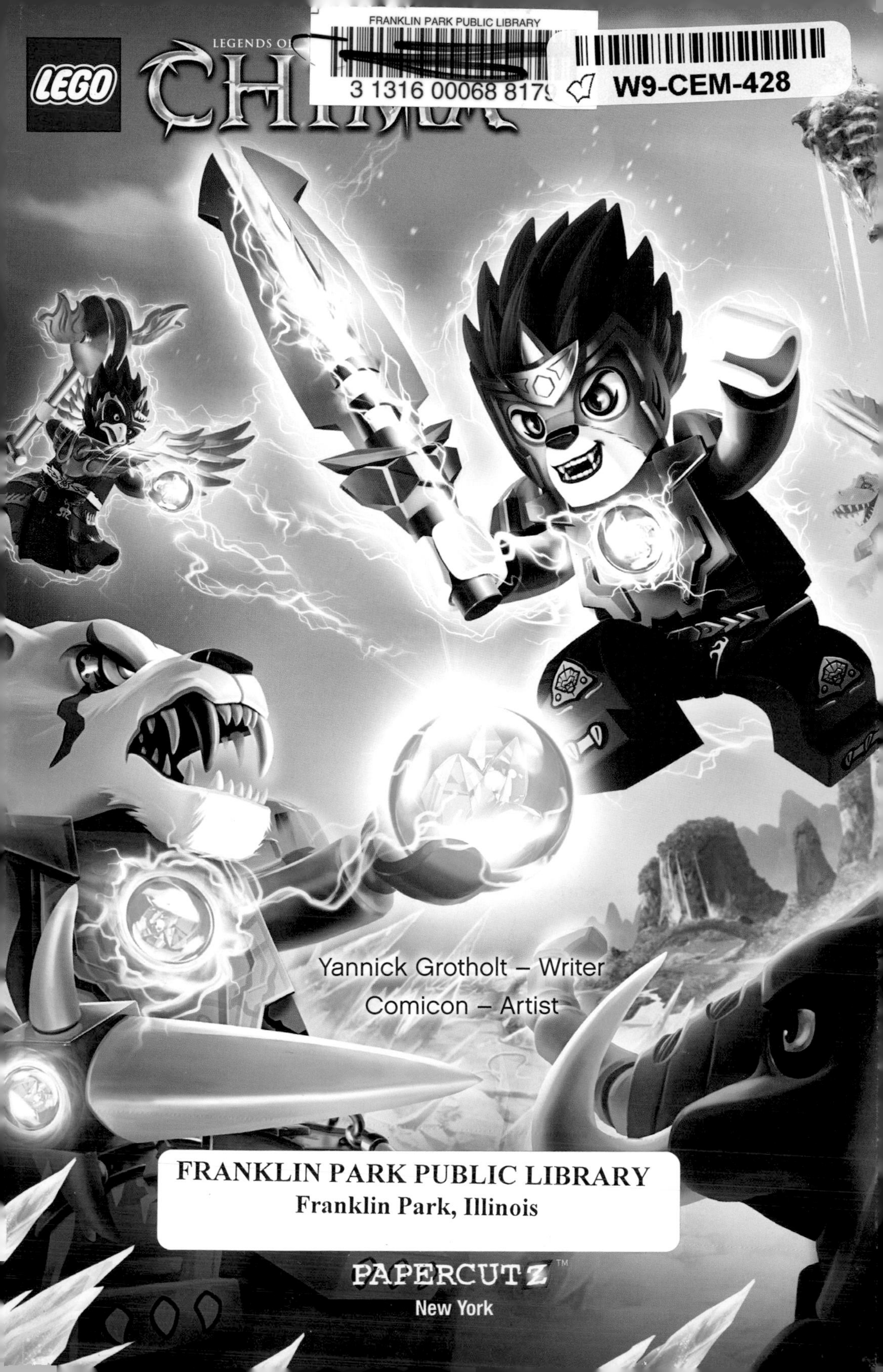

Yannick Grotholt – Writer
Comicon – Artist

PAPERCUTZ™
New York

 CHIMA™ Graphic Novels Available from PAPERCUTZ™

Graphic Novel #1
"High Risk!"

Graphic Novel #2
"The Right Decision"

Graphic Novel #3
"CHI Quest!"

Graphic Novel #4
"The Power of Fire Chi"

Graphic Novel #5
"Wings for a Lion"

J-GN
LEGO LEGENDS OF CHIMA
068-8179

FSC
www.fsc.org
MIX
Paper from
responsible sources
FSC® C006398

LEGO LEGENDS OF CHIMA graphic novels are available for $7.99 in paperback, $12.99. Available from booksellers everywhere. You can also order online from Papercutz.com. Or call 1-800-886-1223, Monday through Friday, 9-5 EST. MC, Visa, and AmEx accepted. To order by mail, please add $4.00 for postage and handling for first book ordered, $1.00 for each additional book and make check payable to NBM Publishing. Send to: Papercutz, 160 Broadway, Suite 700, East Wing, New York, NY 10039.

LEGO LEGENDS OF CHIMA graphic novels are also available digitally wherever e-books are sold.

Papercutz.com

LEGO LEGENDS OF CHIMA
#5 "Wings for a Lion"

Yannick Grotholt — Writer
Comicon — Artist
Tom Orzechowski — Letterer
Dan Berlin, Dani Breckenridge — Editorial Interns
Jeff Whitman — Production Coordinator
Bethany Bryan — Associate Editor
Jim Salicrup
Editor-in-Chief

ISBN: 978-1-62991-184-7 paperback edition
ISBN: 978-1-62991-185-4 hardcover edition

Printed in Hong Kong
September 2015 by Asia One Printing LTD
13/F Asia One Tower
8 Fung Yip St., Chaiwan
Hong Kong

Papercutz books may be purchased for business or promotional use. For information on bulk purchases please contact Macmillan Corporate and Premium Sales Department at (800) 221-7945 x5442.

Distributed by Macmillan
First Papercutz Printing

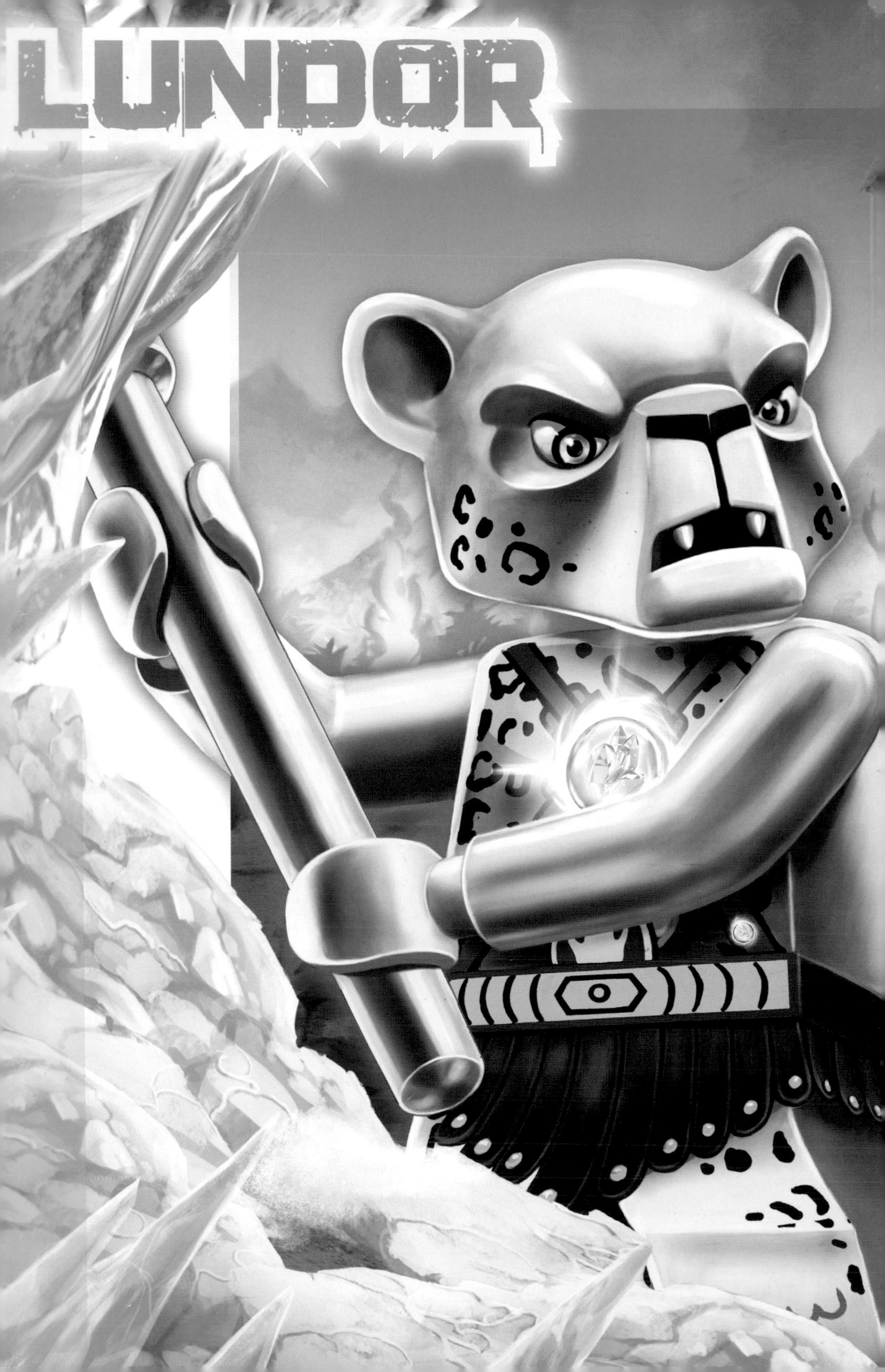
LUNDOR

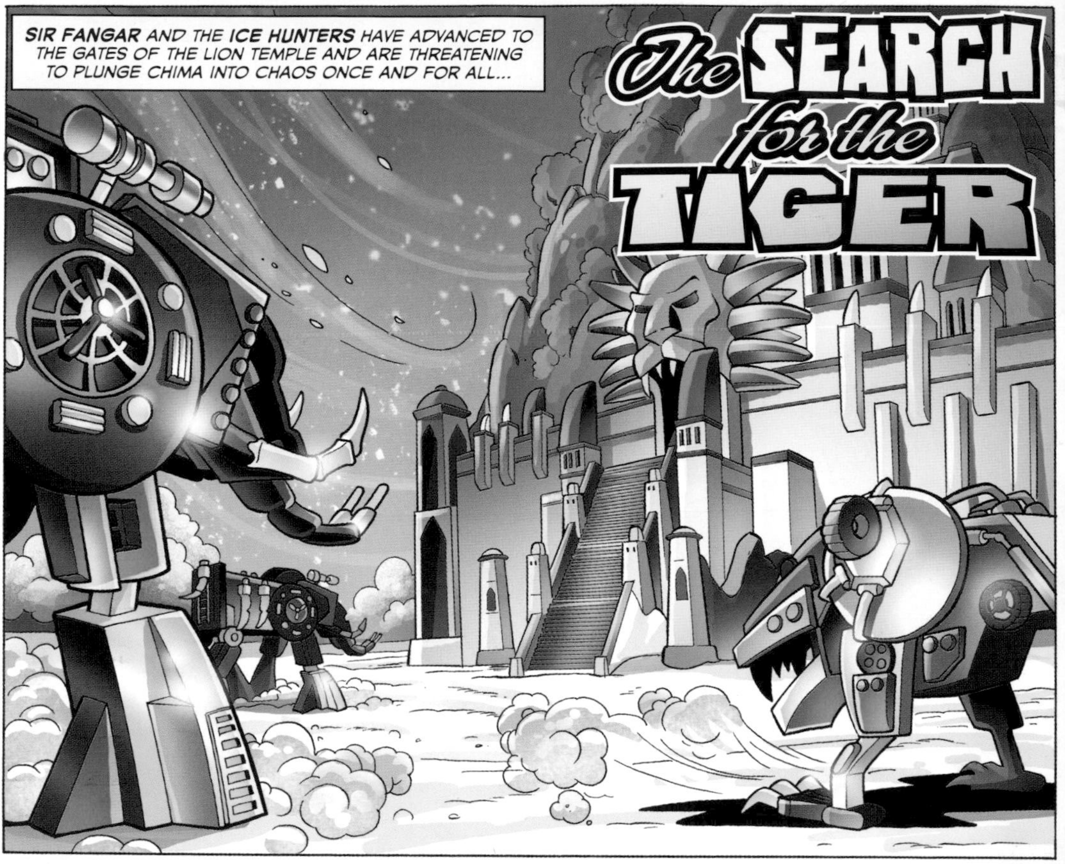
SIR FANGAR AND THE ICE HUNTERS HAVE ADVANCED TO THE GATES OF THE LION TEMPLE AND ARE THREATENING TO PLUNGE CHIMA INTO CHAOS ONCE AND FOR ALL...
The SEARCH for the TIGER

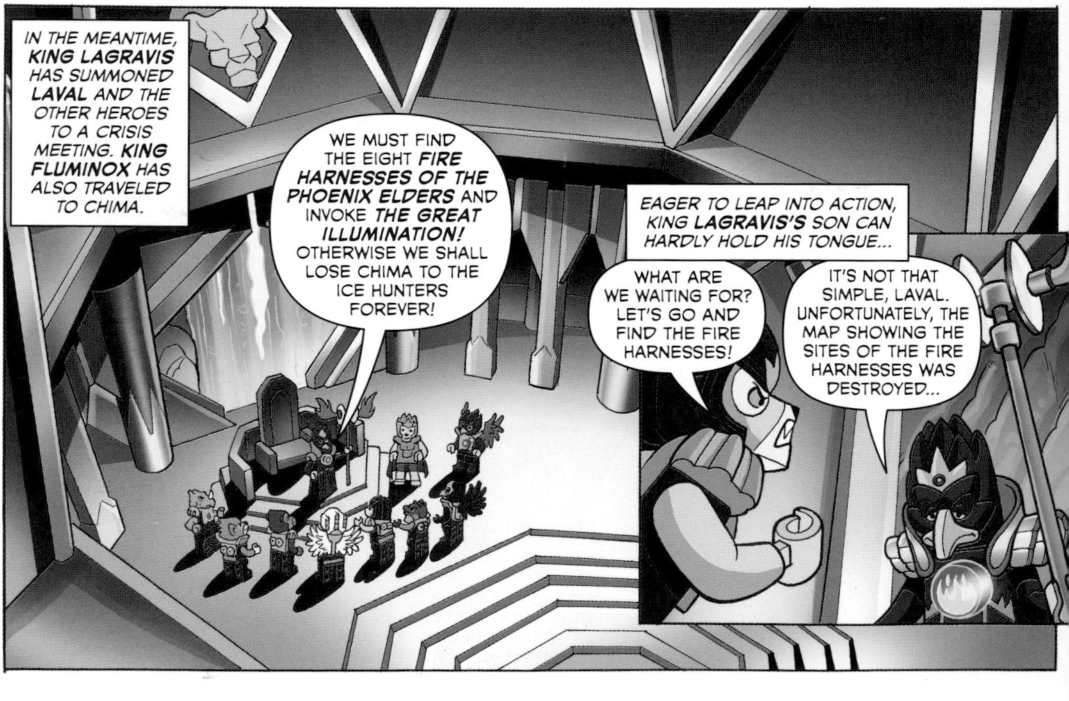
IN THE MEANTIME, KING LAGRAVIS HAS SUMMONED LAVAL AND THE OTHER HEROES TO A CRISIS MEETING. KING FLUMINOX HAS ALSO TRAVELED TO CHIMA.
WE MUST FIND THE EIGHT FIRE HARNESSES OF THE PHOENIX ELDERS AND INVOKE THE GREAT ILLUMINATION! OTHERWISE WE SHALL LOSE CHIMA TO THE ICE HUNTERS FOREVER!
EAGER TO LEAP INTO ACTION, KING LAGRAVIS'S SON CAN HARDLY HOLD HIS TONGUE...
WHAT ARE WE WAITING FOR? LET'S GO AND FIND THE FIRE HARNESSES!
IT'S NOT THAT SIMPLE, LAVAL. UNFORTUNATELY, THE MAP SHOWING THE SITES OF THE FIRE HARNESSES WAS DESTROYED...

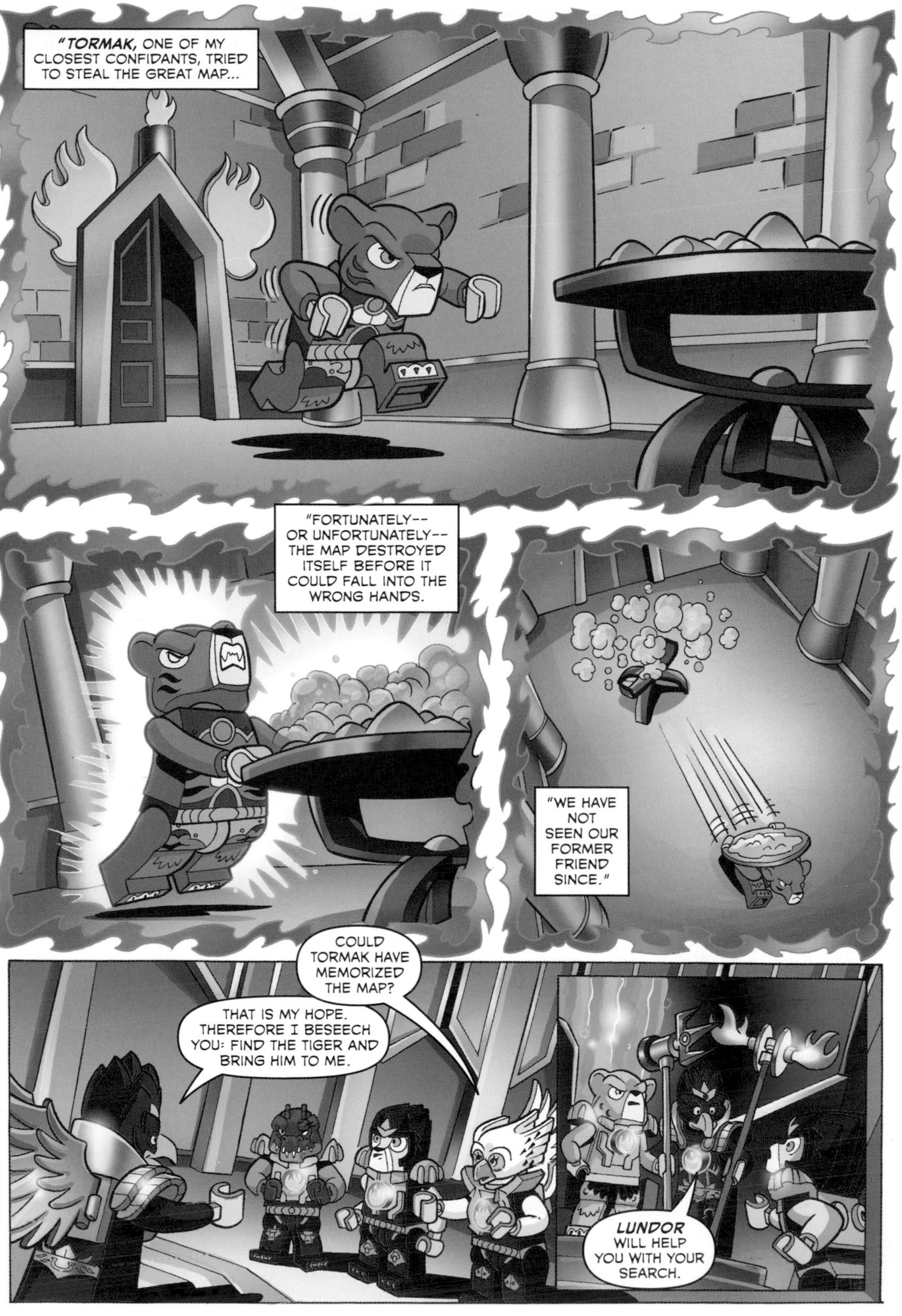
"TORMAK, ONE OF MY CLOSEST CONFIDANTS, TRIED TO STEAL THE GREAT MAP...
"FORTUNATELY-- OR UNFORTUNATELY-- THE MAP DESTROYED ITSELF BEFORE IT COULD FALL INTO THE WRONG HANDS.
"WE HAVE NOT SEEN OUR FORMER FRIEND SINCE."
COULD TORMAK HAVE MEMORIZED THE MAP?
THAT IS MY HOPE. THEREFORE I BESEECH YOU: FIND THE TIGER AND BRING HIM TO ME.
LUNDOR WILL HELP YOU WITH YOUR SEARCH.

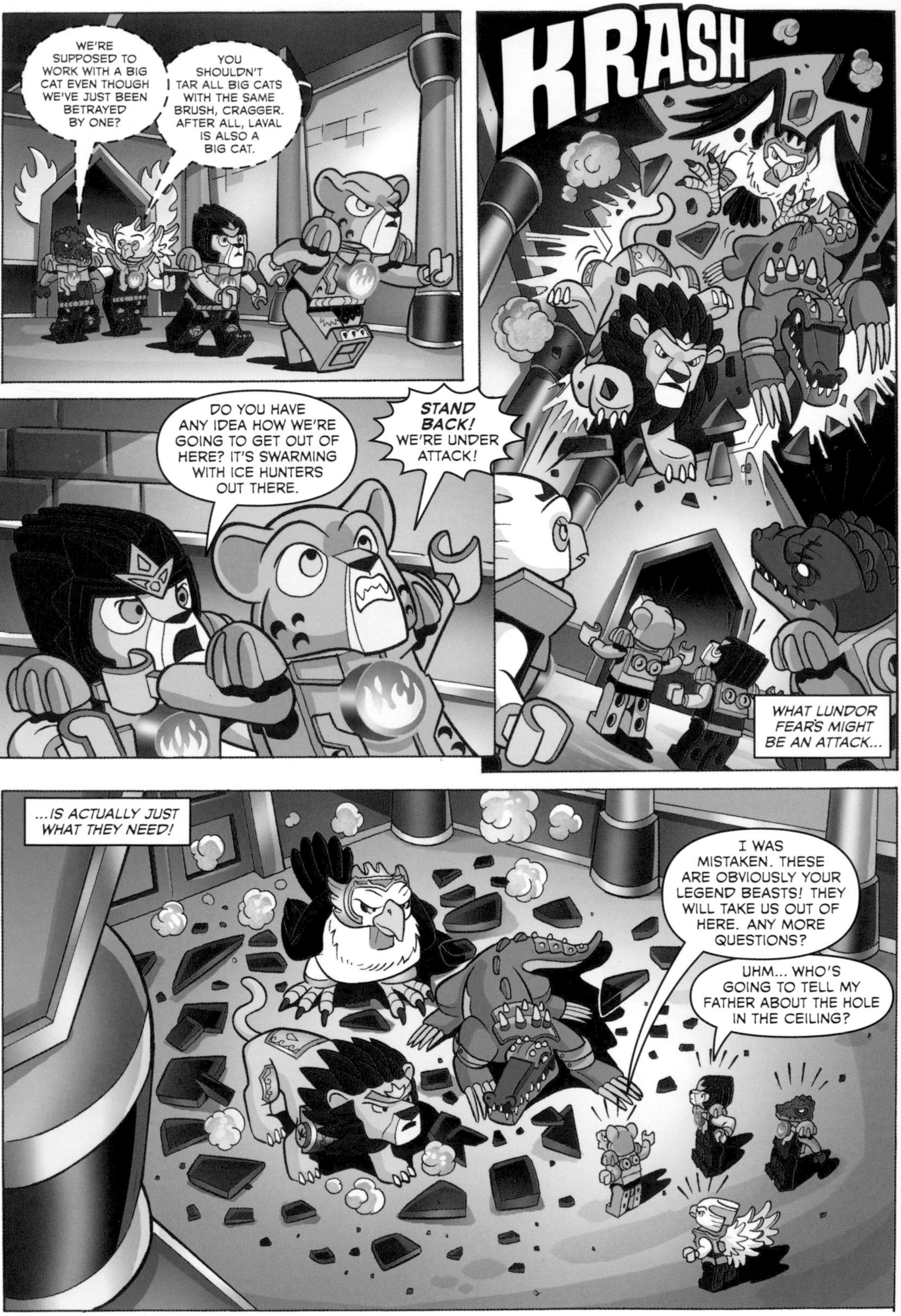
WE'RE SUPPOSED TO WORK WITH A BIG CAT EVEN THOUGH WE'VE JUST BEEN BETRAYED BY ONE?
YOU SHOULDN'T TAR ALL BIG CATS WITH THE SAME BRUSH, CRAGGER. AFTER ALL, LAVAL IS ALSO A BIG CAT.
DO YOU HAVE ANY IDEA HOW WE'RE GOING TO GET OUT OF HERE? IT'S SWARMING WITH ICE HUNTERS OUT THERE.
STAND BACK! WE'RE UNDER ATTACK!
KRASH
WHAT LUNDOR FEAR'S MIGHT BE AN ATTACK...
...IS ACTUALLY JUST WHAT THEY NEED!
I WAS MISTAKEN. THESE ARE OBVIOUSLY YOUR LEGEND BEASTS! THEY WILL TAKE US OUT OF HERE. ANY MORE QUESTIONS?
UHM... WHO'S GOING TO TELL MY FATHER ABOUT THE HOLE IN THE CEILING?

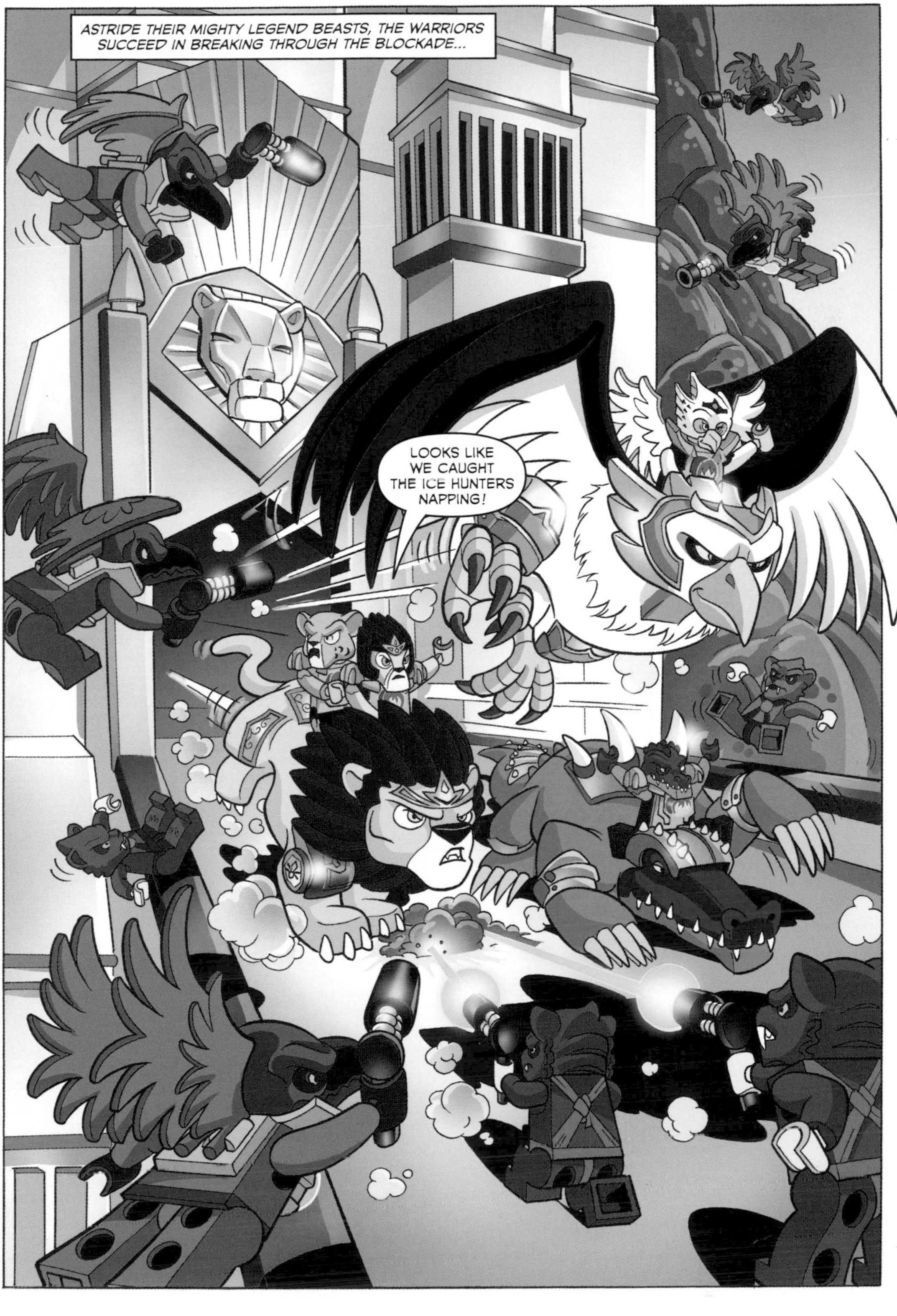
ASTRIDE THEIR MIGHTY LEGEND BEASTS, THE WARRIORS SUCCEED IN BREAKING THROUGH THE BLOCKADE...
LOOKS LIKE WE CAUGHT THE ICE HUNTERS NAPPING!

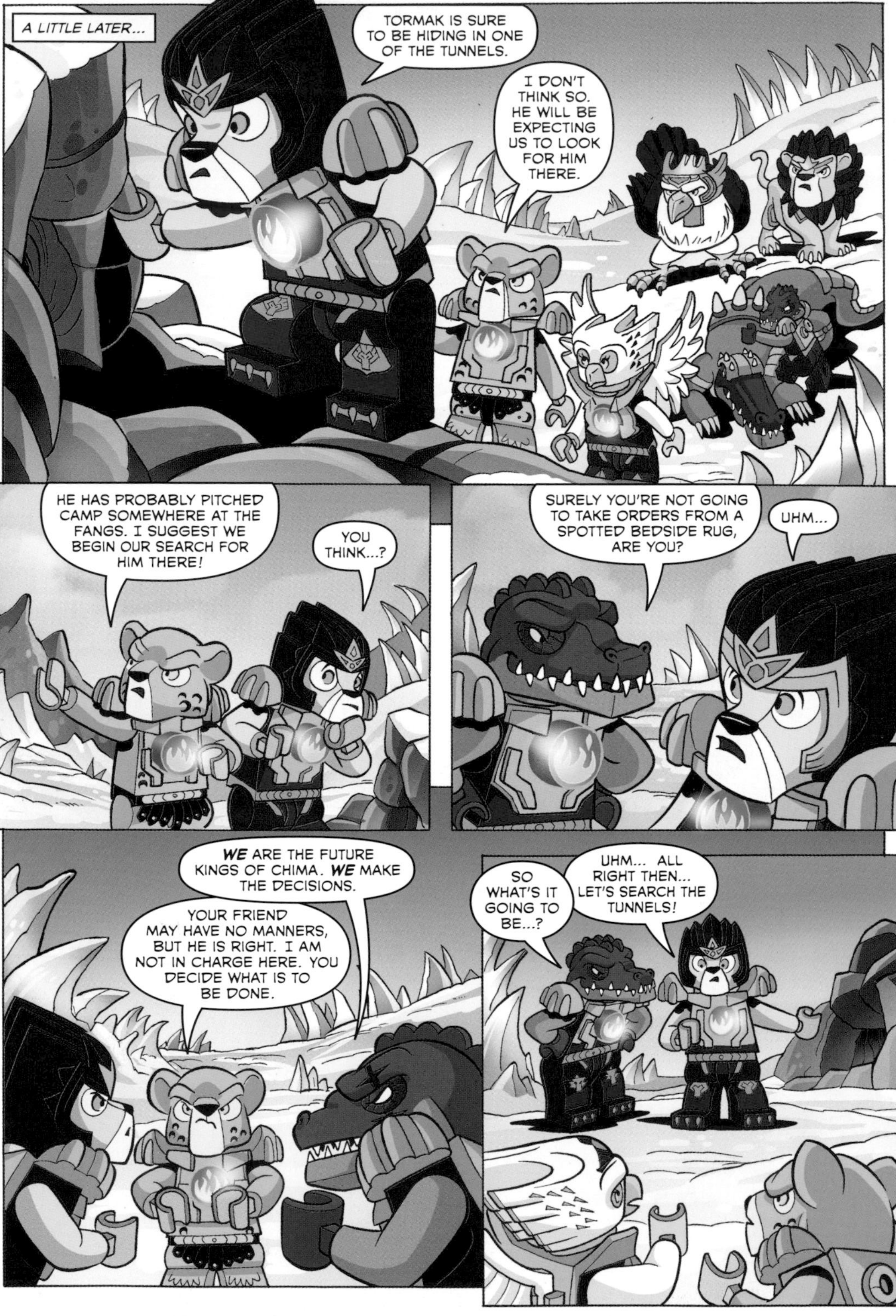
A LITTLE LATER...
TORMAK IS SURE TO BE HIDING IN ONE OF THE TUNNELS.
I DON'T THINK SO. HE WILL BE EXPECTING US TO LOOK FOR HIM THERE.
HE HAS PROBABLY PITCHED CAMP SOMEWHERE AT THE FANGS. I SUGGEST WE BEGIN OUR SEARCH FOR HIM THERE!
YOU THINK...?
SURELY YOU'RE NOT GOING TO TAKE ORDERS FROM A SPOTTED BEDSIDE RUG, ARE YOU?
UHM...
WE ARE THE FUTURE KINGS OF CHIMA. *WE* MAKE THE DECISIONS.
YOUR FRIEND MAY HAVE NO MANNERS, BUT HE IS RIGHT. I AM NOT IN CHARGE HERE. YOU DECIDE WHAT IS TO BE DONE.
SO WHAT'S IT GOING TO BE...?
UHM... ALL RIGHT THEN... LET'S SEARCH THE TUNNELS!

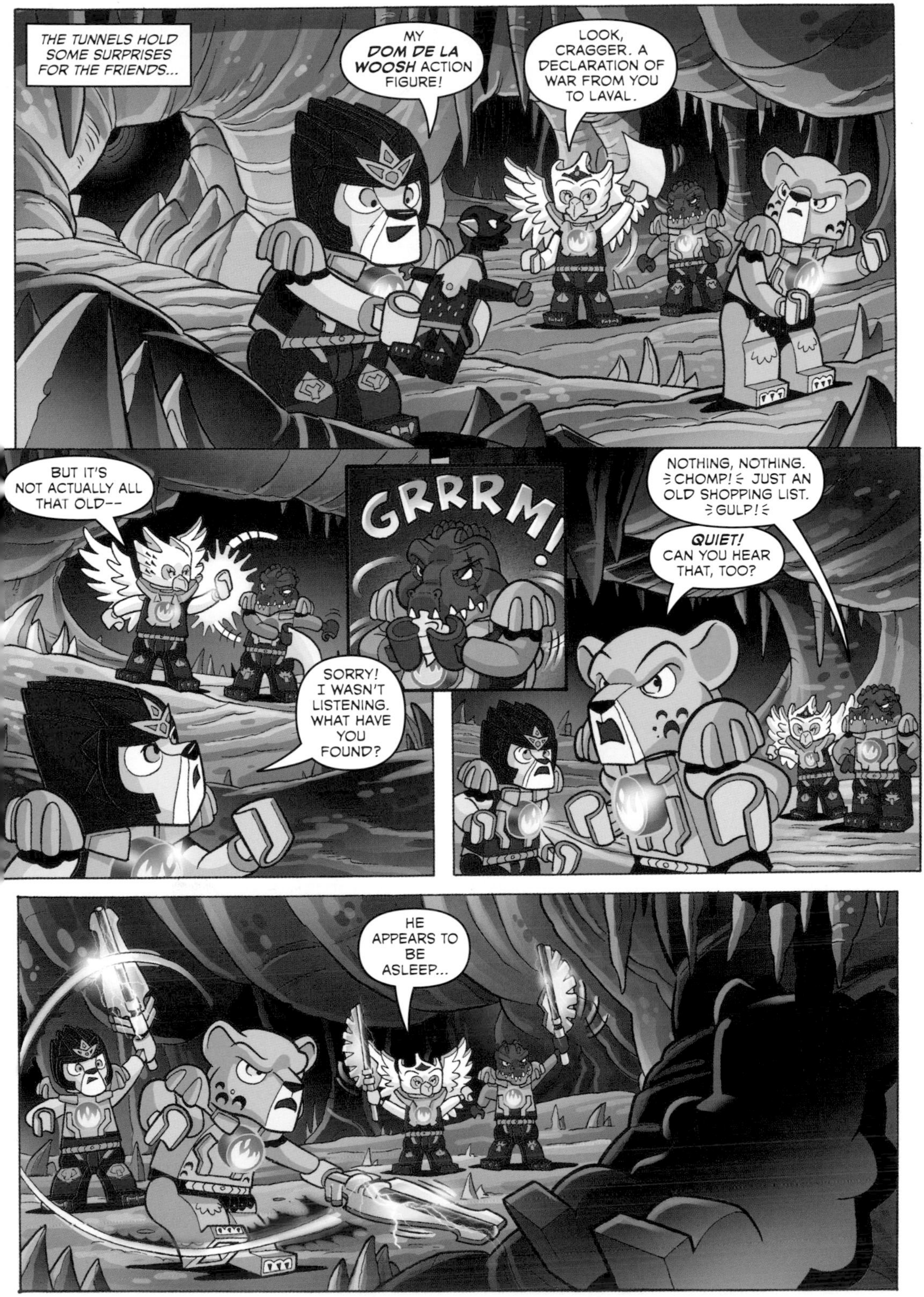
THE TUNNELS HOLD SOME SURPRISES FOR THE FRIENDS...
MY DOM DE LA WOOSH ACTION FIGURE!
LOOK, CRAGGER. A DECLARATION OF WAR FROM YOU TO LAVAL.
BUT IT'S NOT ACTUALLY ALL THAT OLD--
GRRRM!
SORRY! I WASN'T LISTENING. WHAT HAVE YOU FOUND?
NOTHING, NOTHING. CHOMP! JUST AN OLD SHOPPING LIST. GULP!
QUIET! CAN YOU HEAR THAT, TOO?
HE APPEARS TO BE ASLEEP...

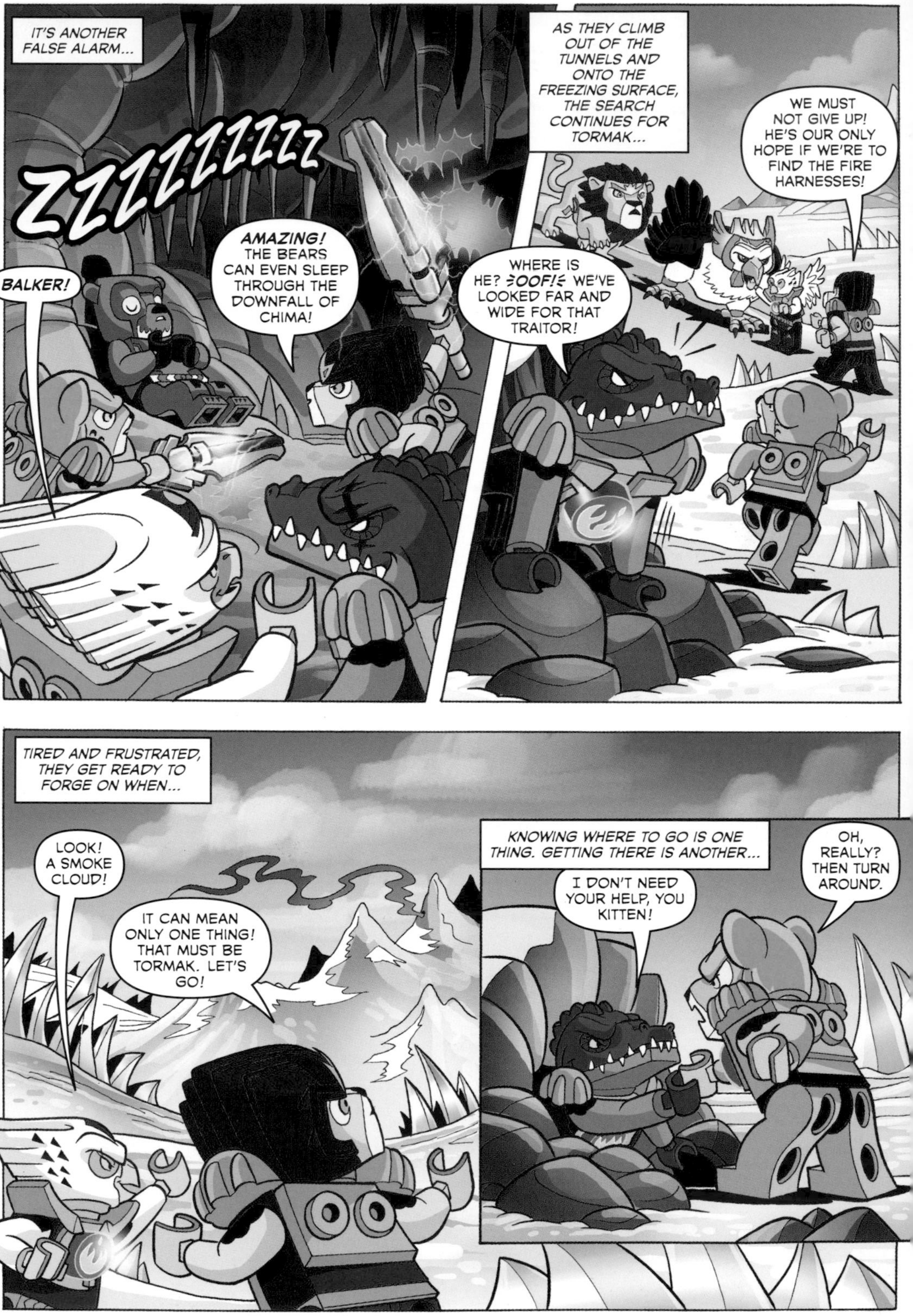
IT'S ANOTHER FALSE ALARM...
ZZZZZZZZZZZ
BALKER!
AMAZING! THE BEARS CAN EVEN SLEEP THROUGH THE DOWNFALL OF CHIMA!
AS THEY CLIMB OUT OF THE TUNNELS AND ONTO THE FREEZING SURFACE, THE SEARCH CONTINUES FOR TORMAK...
WE MUST NOT GIVE UP! HE'S OUR ONLY HOPE IF WE'RE TO FIND THE FIRE HARNESSES!
WHERE IS HE? OOF! WE'VE LOOKED FAR AND WIDE FOR THAT TRAITOR!
TIRED AND FRUSTRATED, THEY GET READY TO FORGE ON WHEN...
LOOK! A SMOKE CLOUD!
IT CAN MEAN ONLY ONE THING! THAT MUST BE TORMAK. LET'S GO!
KNOWING WHERE TO GO IS ONE THING. GETTING THERE IS ANOTHER...
I DON'T NEED YOUR HELP, YOU KITTEN!
OH, REALLY? THEN TURN AROUND.

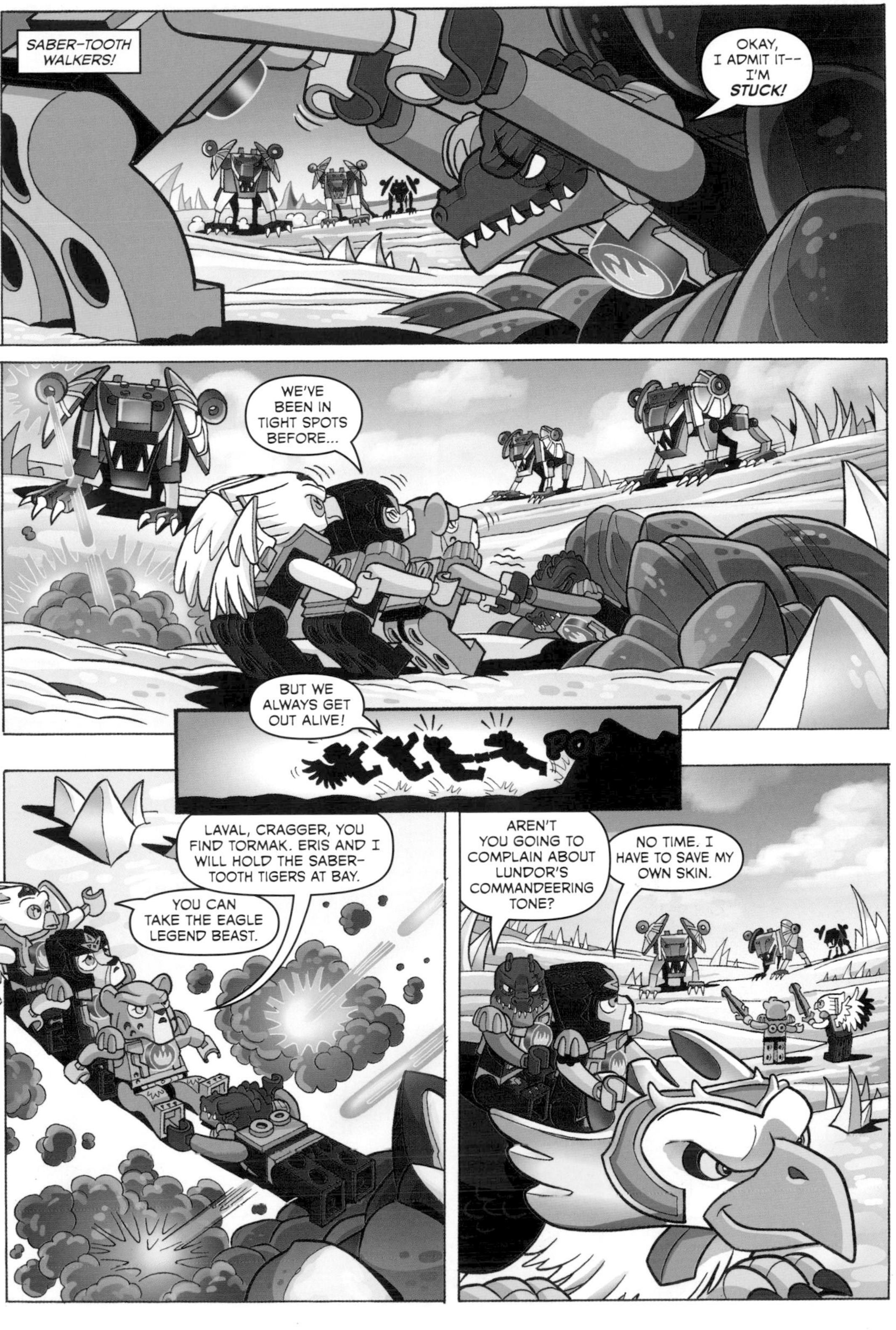
SABER-TOOTH WALKERS!
OKAY, I ADMIT IT-- I'M **STUCK!**
WE'VE BEEN IN TIGHT SPOTS BEFORE...
BUT WE ALWAYS GET OUT ALIVE!
POP
LAVAL, CRAGGER, YOU FIND TORMAK. ERIS AND I WILL HOLD THE SABER-TOOTH TIGERS AT BAY.
YOU CAN TAKE THE EAGLE LEGEND BEAST.
AREN'T YOU GOING TO COMPLAIN ABOUT LUNDOR'S COMMANDEERING TONE?
NO TIME. I HAVE TO SAVE MY OWN SKIN.

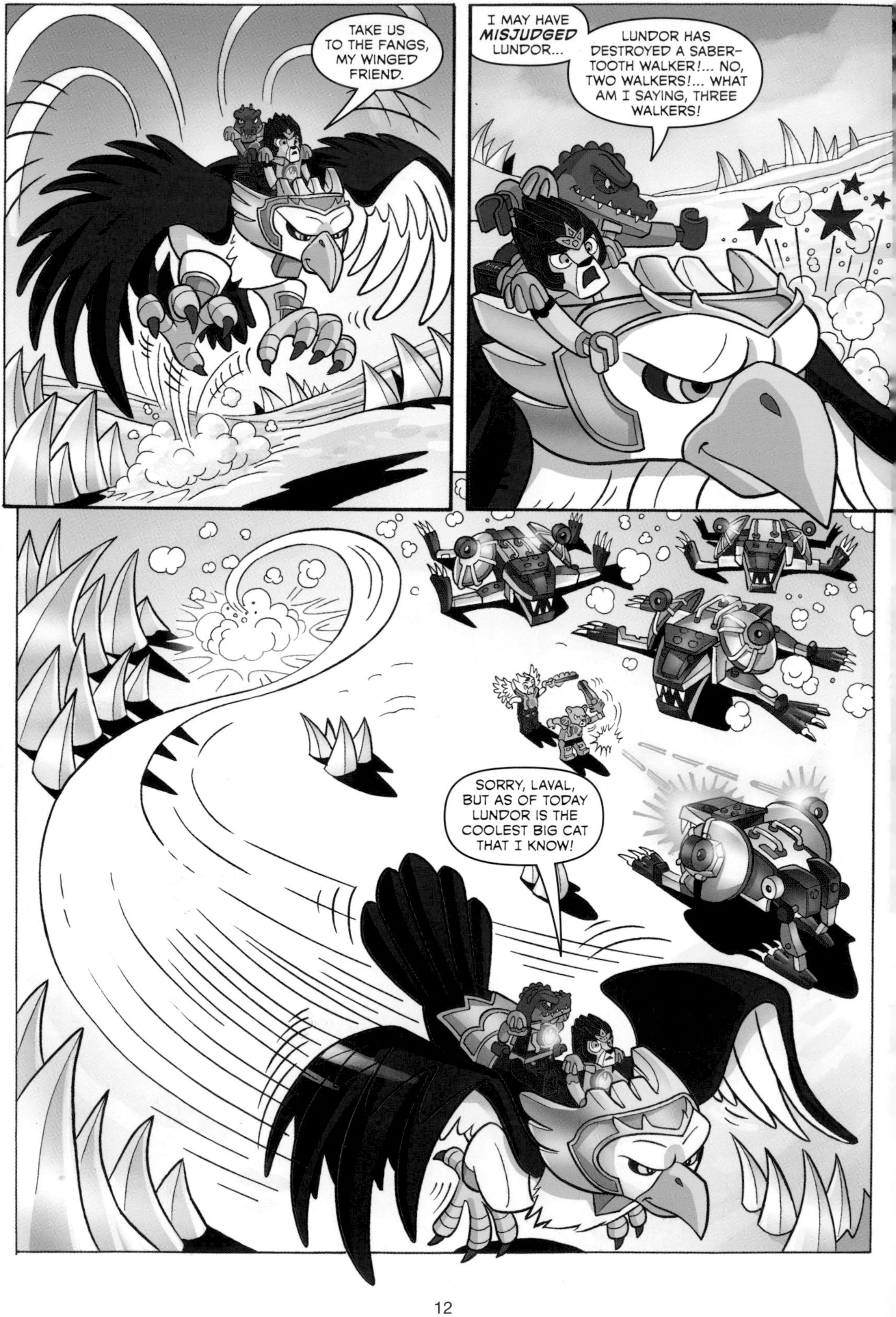
TAKE US TO THE FANGS, MY WINGED FRIEND.
I MAY HAVE MISJUDGED LUNDOR...
LUNDOR HAS DESTROYED A SABER-TOOTH WALKER!... NO, TWO WALKERS!... WHAT AM I SAYING, THREE WALKERS!
SORRY, LAVAL, BUT AS OF TODAY LUNDOR IS THE COOLEST BIG CAT THAT I KNOW!

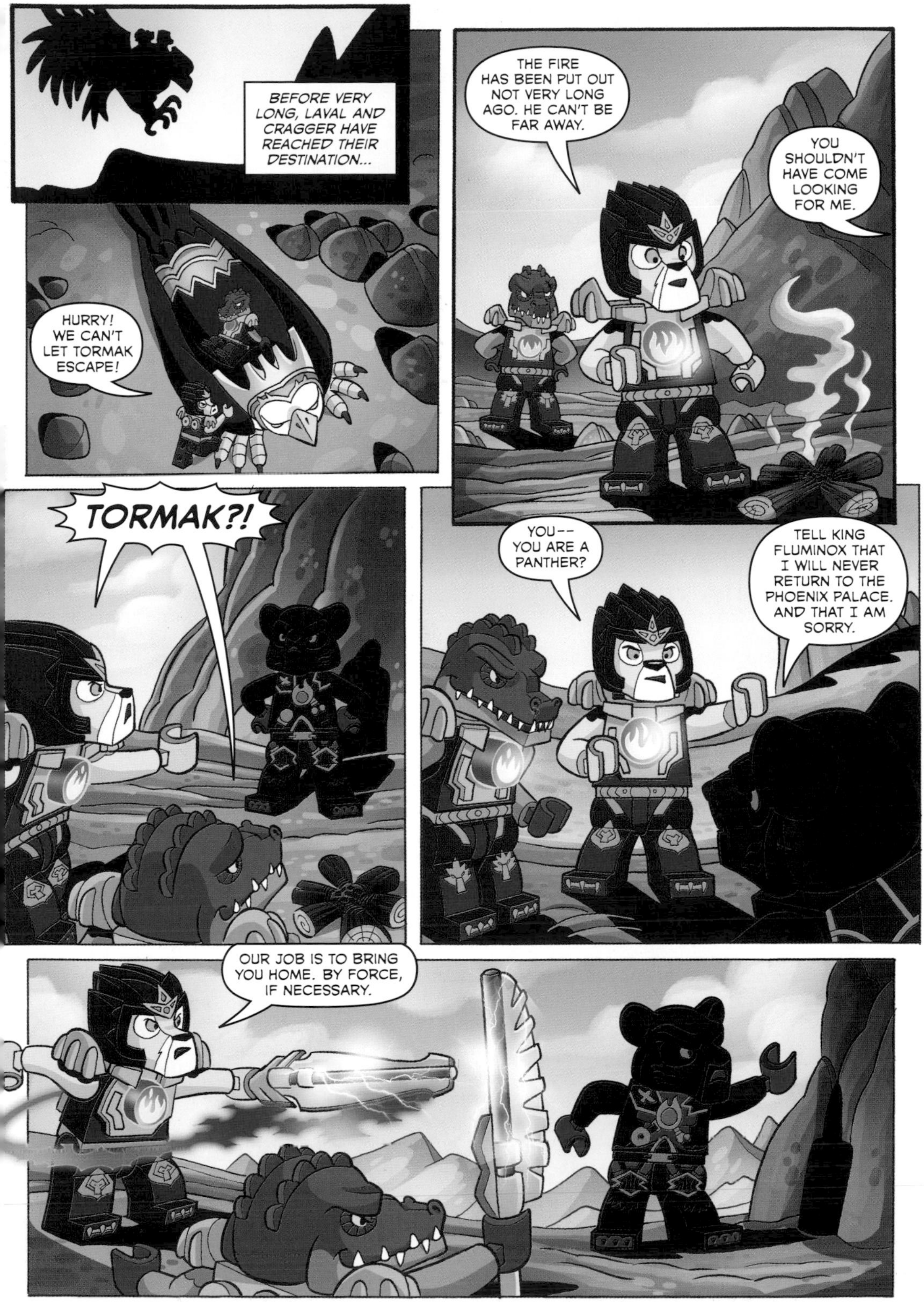
BEFORE VERY LONG, LAVAL AND CRAGGER HAVE REACHED THEIR DESTINATION...
HURRY! WE CAN'T LET TORMAK ESCAPE!
THE FIRE HAS BEEN PUT OUT NOT VERY LONG AGO. HE CAN'T BE FAR AWAY.
YOU SHOULDN'T HAVE COME LOOKING FOR ME.
TORMAK?!
YOU-- YOU ARE A PANTHER?
TELL KING FLUMINOX THAT I WILL NEVER RETURN TO THE PHOENIX PALACE. AND THAT I AM SORRY.
OUR JOB IS TO BRING YOU HOME. BY FORCE, IF NECESSARY.

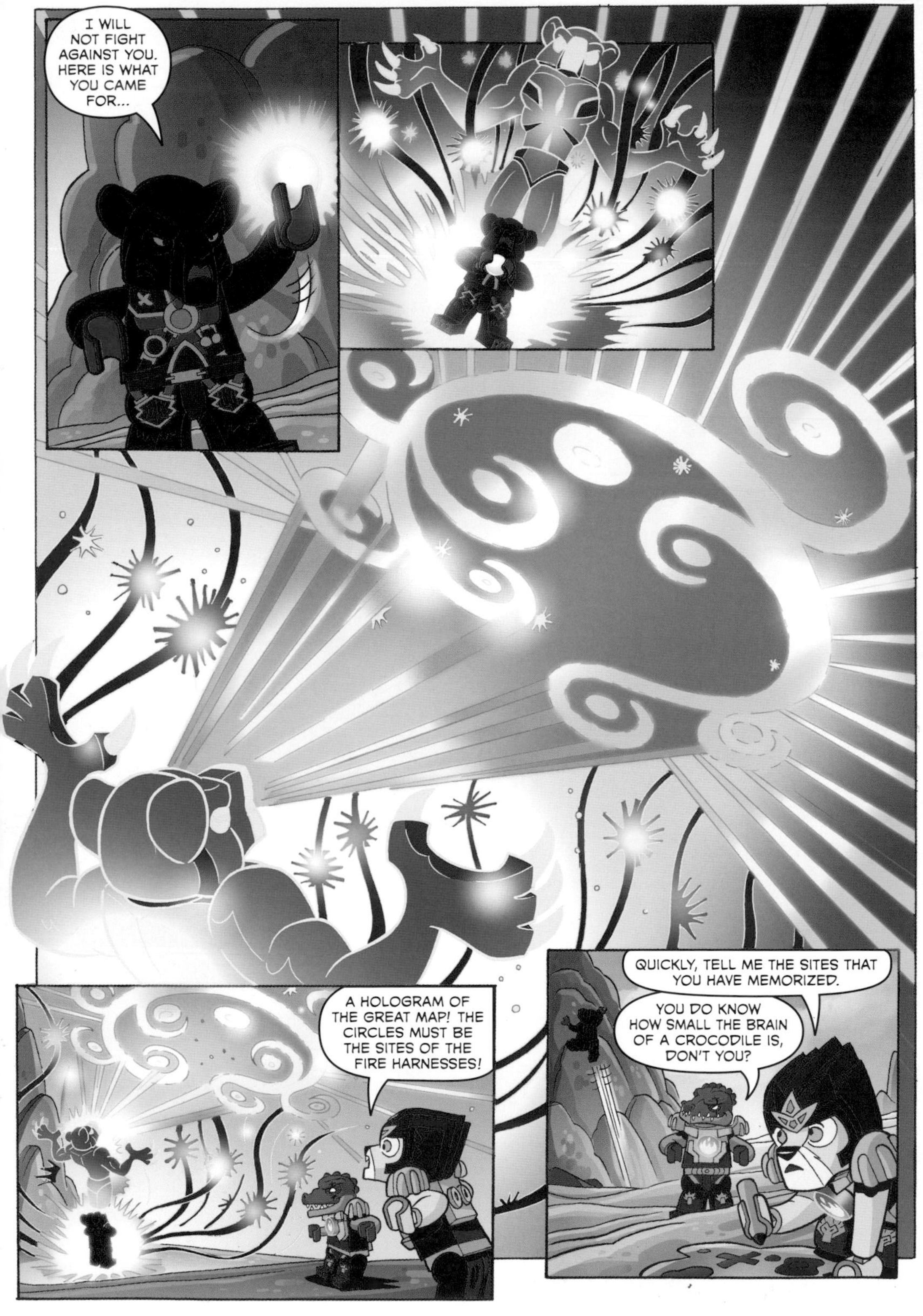
I WILL NOT FIGHT AGAINST YOU. HERE IS WHAT YOU CAME FOR...
A HOLOGRAM OF THE GREAT MAP! THE CIRCLES MUST BE THE SITES OF THE FIRE HARNESSES!
QUICKLY, TELL ME THE SITES THAT YOU HAVE MEMORIZED.
YOU DO KNOW HOW SMALL THE BRAIN OF A CROCODILE IS, DON'T YOU?

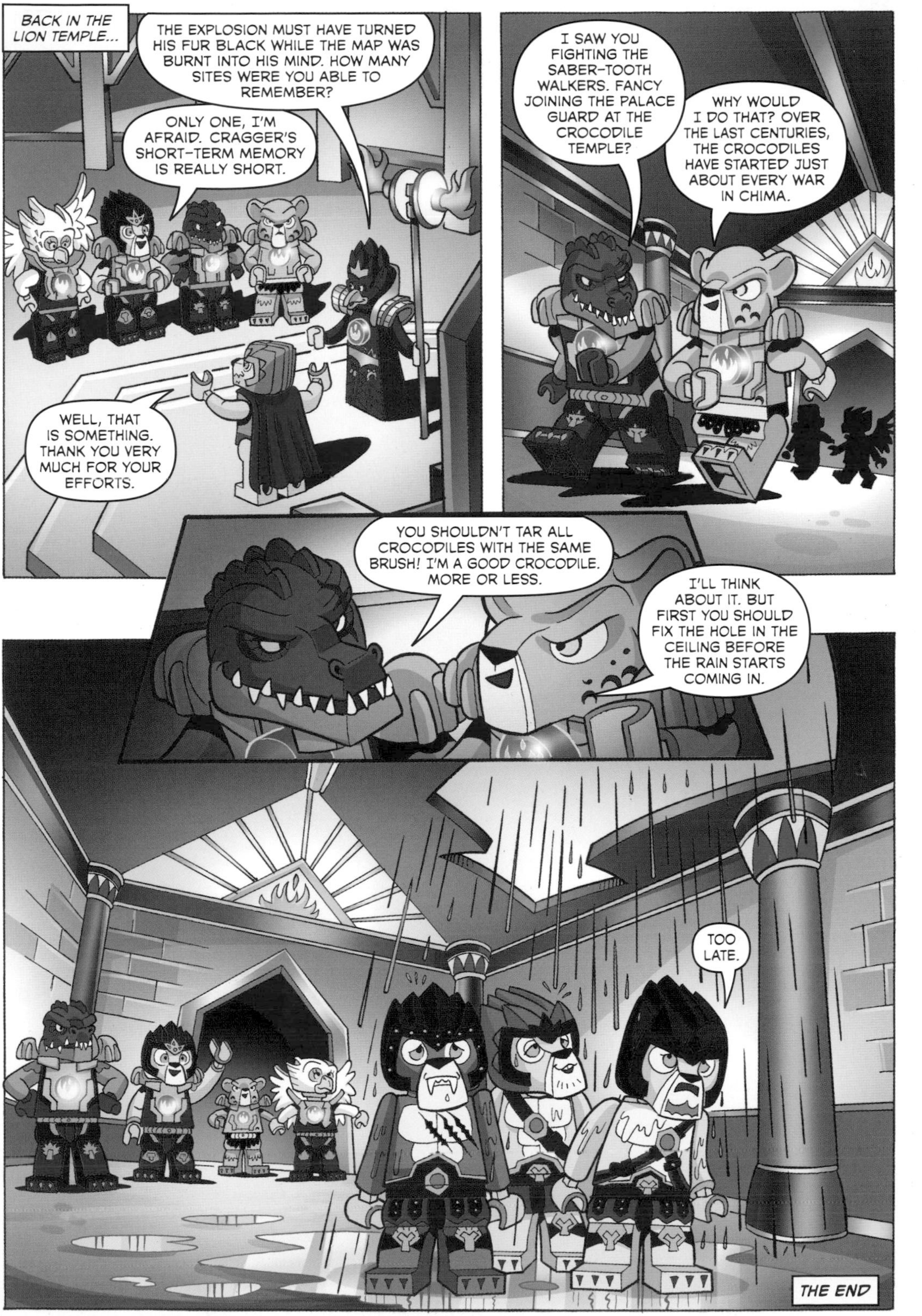
BACK IN THE LION TEMPLE...
THE EXPLOSION MUST HAVE TURNED HIS FUR BLACK WHILE THE MAP WAS BURNT INTO HIS MIND. HOW MANY SITES WERE YOU ABLE TO REMEMBER?
ONLY ONE, I'M AFRAID. CRAGGER'S SHORT-TERM MEMORY IS REALLY SHORT.
WELL, THAT IS SOMETHING. THANK YOU VERY MUCH FOR YOUR EFFORTS.
I SAW YOU FIGHTING THE SABER-TOOTH WALKERS. FANCY JOINING THE PALACE GUARD AT THE CROCODILE TEMPLE?
WHY WOULD I DO THAT? OVER THE LAST CENTURIES, THE CROCODILES HAVE STARTED JUST ABOUT EVERY WAR IN CHIMA.
YOU SHOULDN'T TAR ALL CROCODILES WITH THE SAME BRUSH! I'M A GOOD CROCODILE. MORE OR LESS.
I'LL THINK ABOUT IT. BUT FIRST YOU SHOULD FIX THE HOLE IN THE CEILING BEFORE THE RAIN STARTS COMING IN.
TOO LATE.
THE END

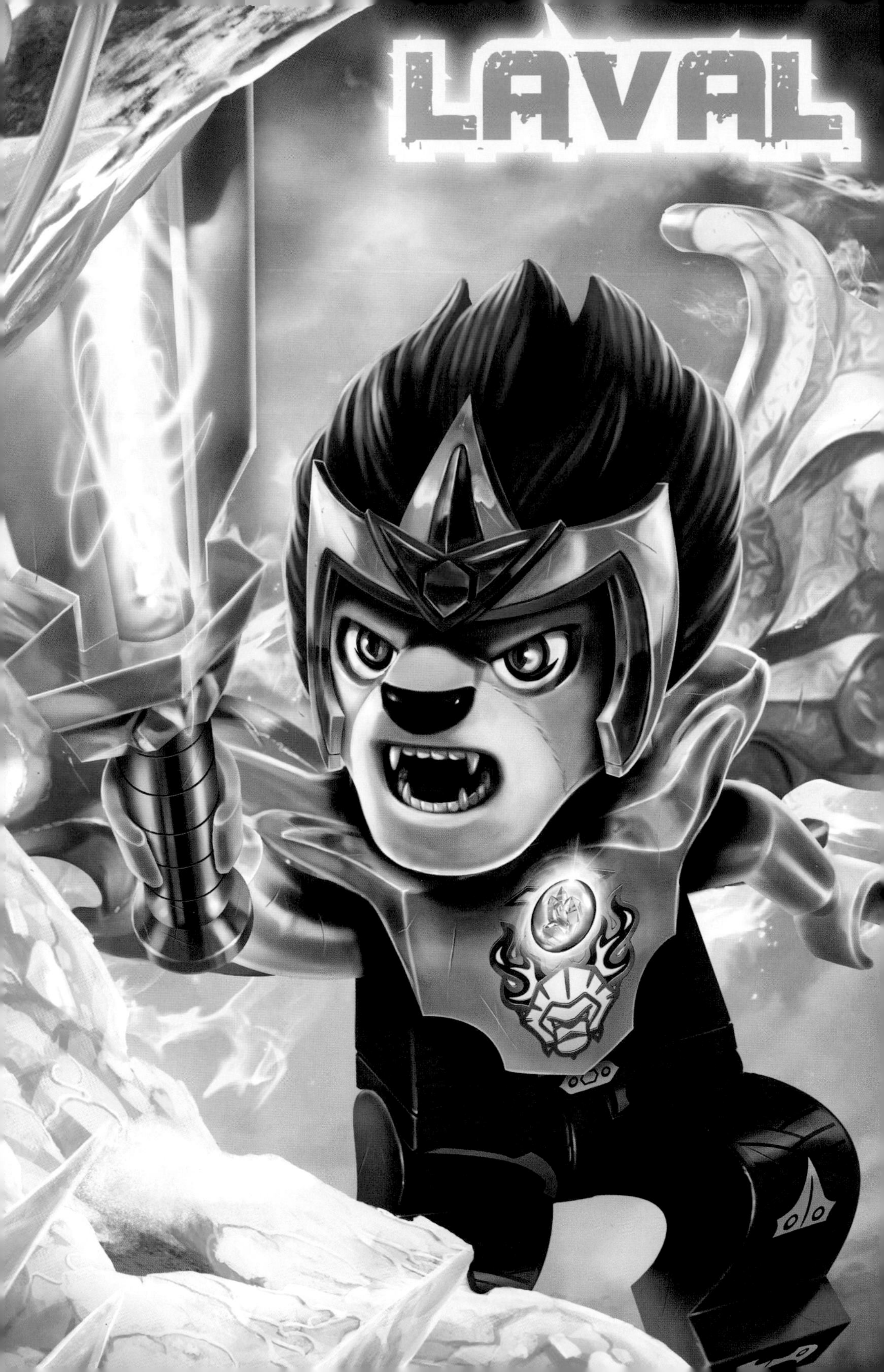
LAVAL

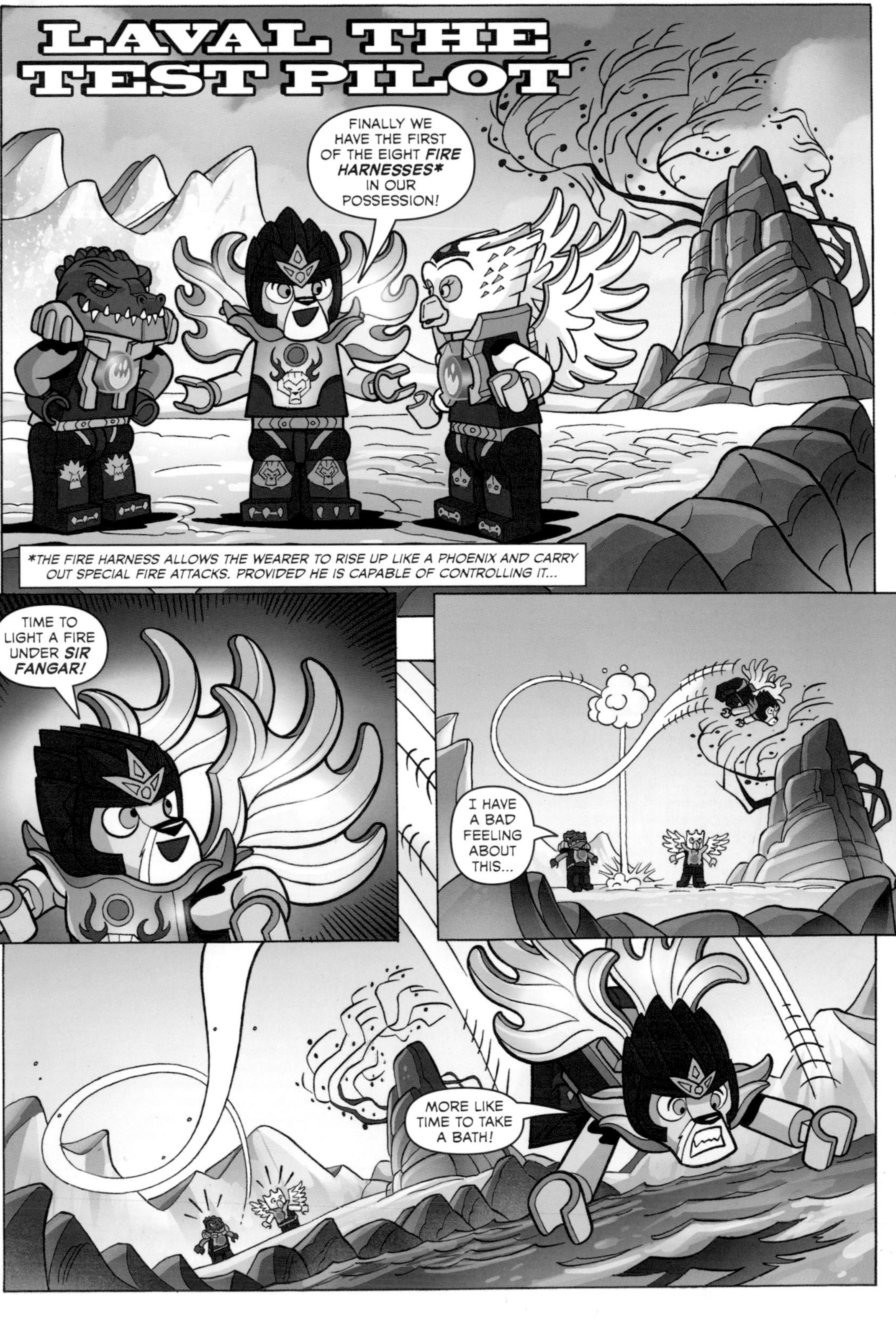
LAVAL THE TEST PILOT
FINALLY WE HAVE THE FIRST OF THE EIGHT FIRE HARNESSES* IN OUR POSSESSION!
*THE FIRE HARNESS ALLOWS THE WEARER TO RISE UP LIKE A PHOENIX AND CARRY OUT SPECIAL FIRE ATTACKS. PROVIDED HE IS CAPABLE OF CONTROLLING IT...
TIME TO LIGHT A FIRE UNDER SIR FANGAR!
I HAVE A BAD FEELING ABOUT THIS...
MORE LIKE TIME TO TAKE A BATH!

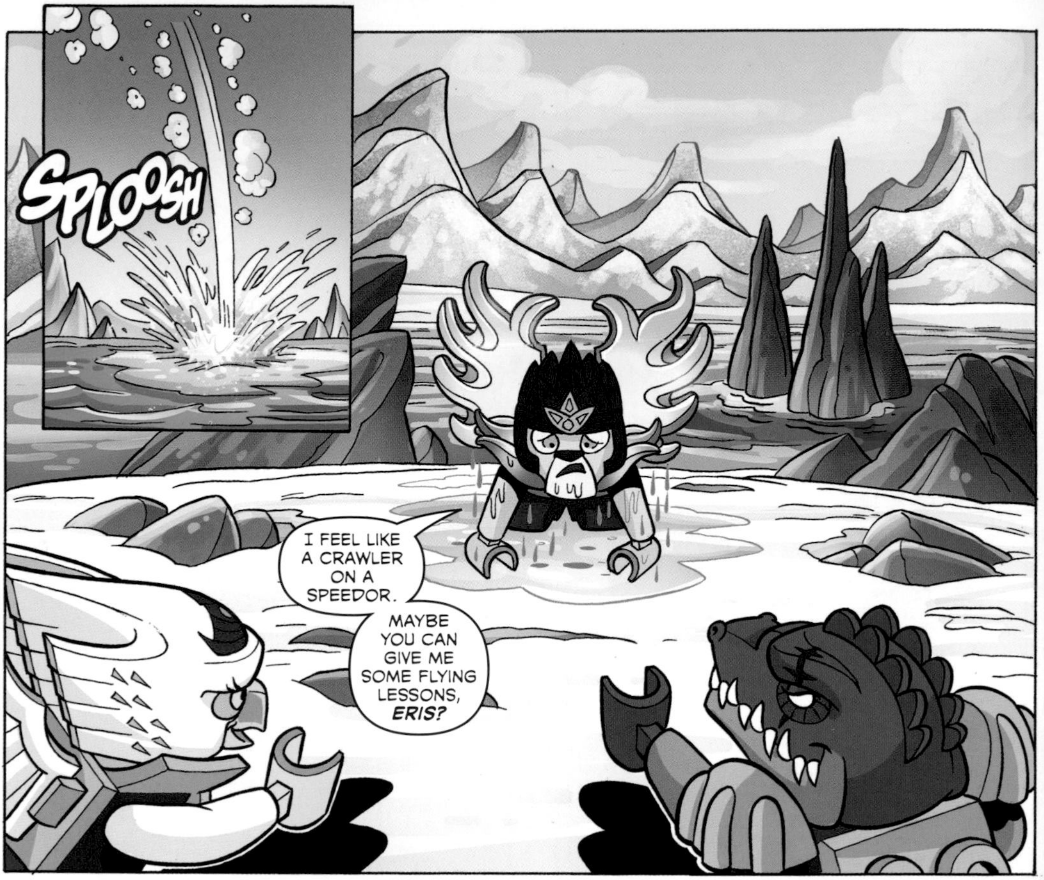
SPLOOSH
I FEEL LIKE A CRAWLER ON A SPEEDOR.
MAYBE YOU CAN GIVE ME SOME FLYING LESSONS, ERIS?

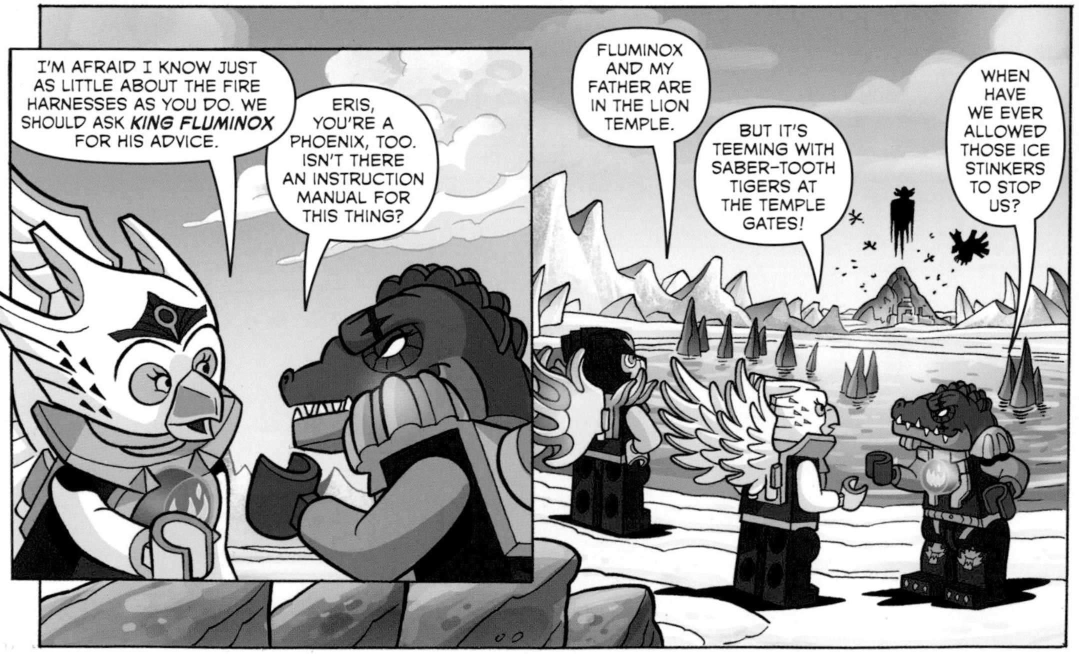
I'M AFRAID I KNOW JUST AS LITTLE ABOUT THE FIRE HARNESSES AS YOU DO. WE SHOULD ASK KING FLUMINOX FOR HIS ADVICE.
ERIS, YOU'RE A PHOENIX, TOO. ISN'T THERE AN INSTRUCTION MANUAL FOR THIS THING?
FLUMINOX AND MY FATHER ARE IN THE LION TEMPLE.
BUT IT'S TEEMING WITH SABER-TOOTH TIGERS AT THE TEMPLE GATES!
WHEN HAVE WE EVER ALLOWED THOSE ICE STINKERS TO STOP US?

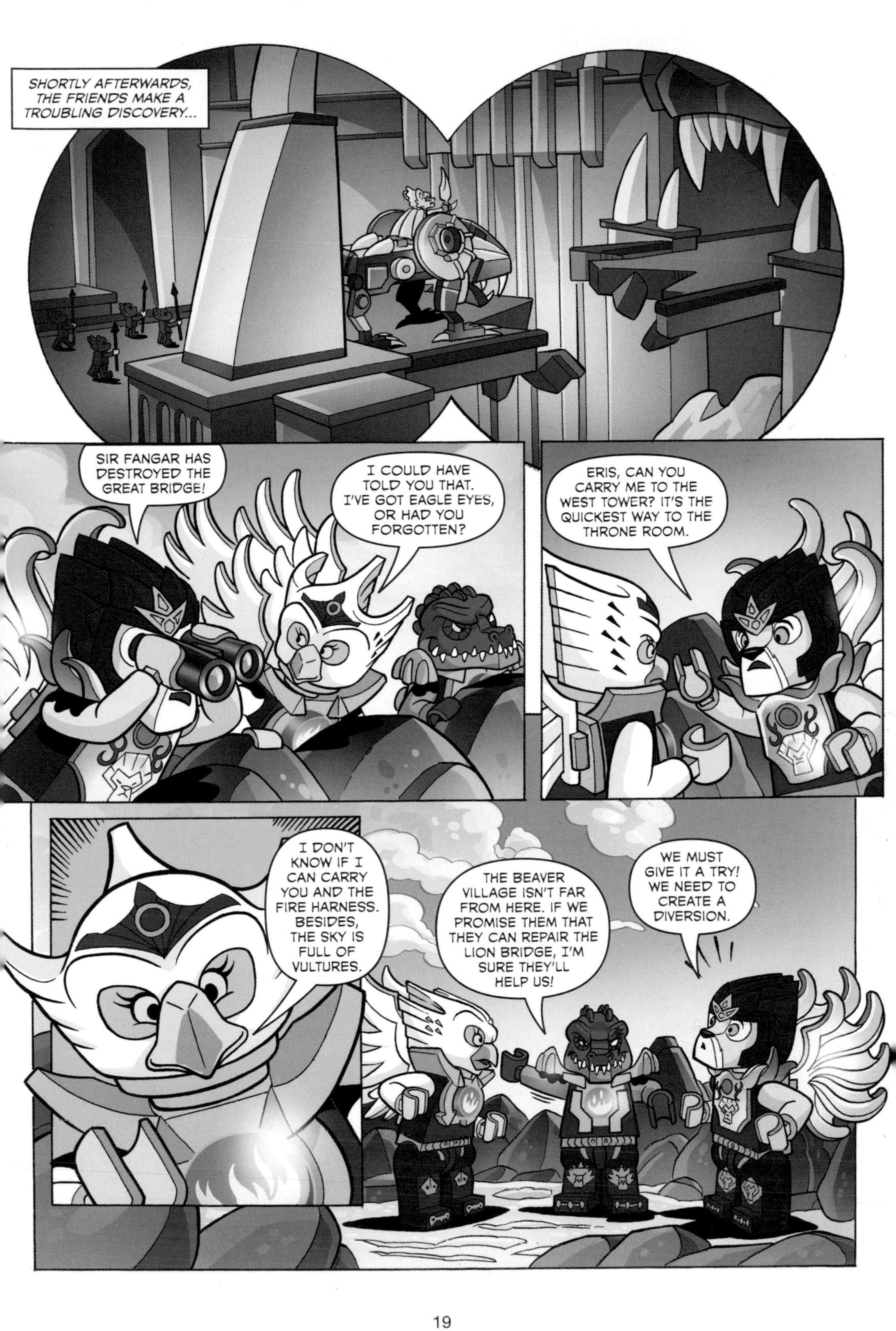
SHORTLY AFTERWARDS, THE FRIENDS MAKE A TROUBLING DISCOVERY...
SIR FANGAR HAS DESTROYED THE GREAT BRIDGE!
I COULD HAVE TOLD YOU THAT. I'VE GOT EAGLE EYES, OR HAD YOU FORGOTTEN?
ERIS, CAN YOU CARRY ME TO THE WEST TOWER? IT'S THE QUICKEST WAY TO THE THRONE ROOM.
I DON'T KNOW IF I CAN CARRY YOU AND THE FIRE HARNESS. BESIDES, THE SKY IS FULL OF VULTURES.
THE BEAVER VILLAGE ISN'T FAR FROM HERE. IF WE PROMISE THEM THAT THEY CAN REPAIR THE LION BRIDGE, I'M SURE THEY'LL HELP US!
WE MUST GIVE IT A TRY! WE NEED TO CREATE A DIVERSION.

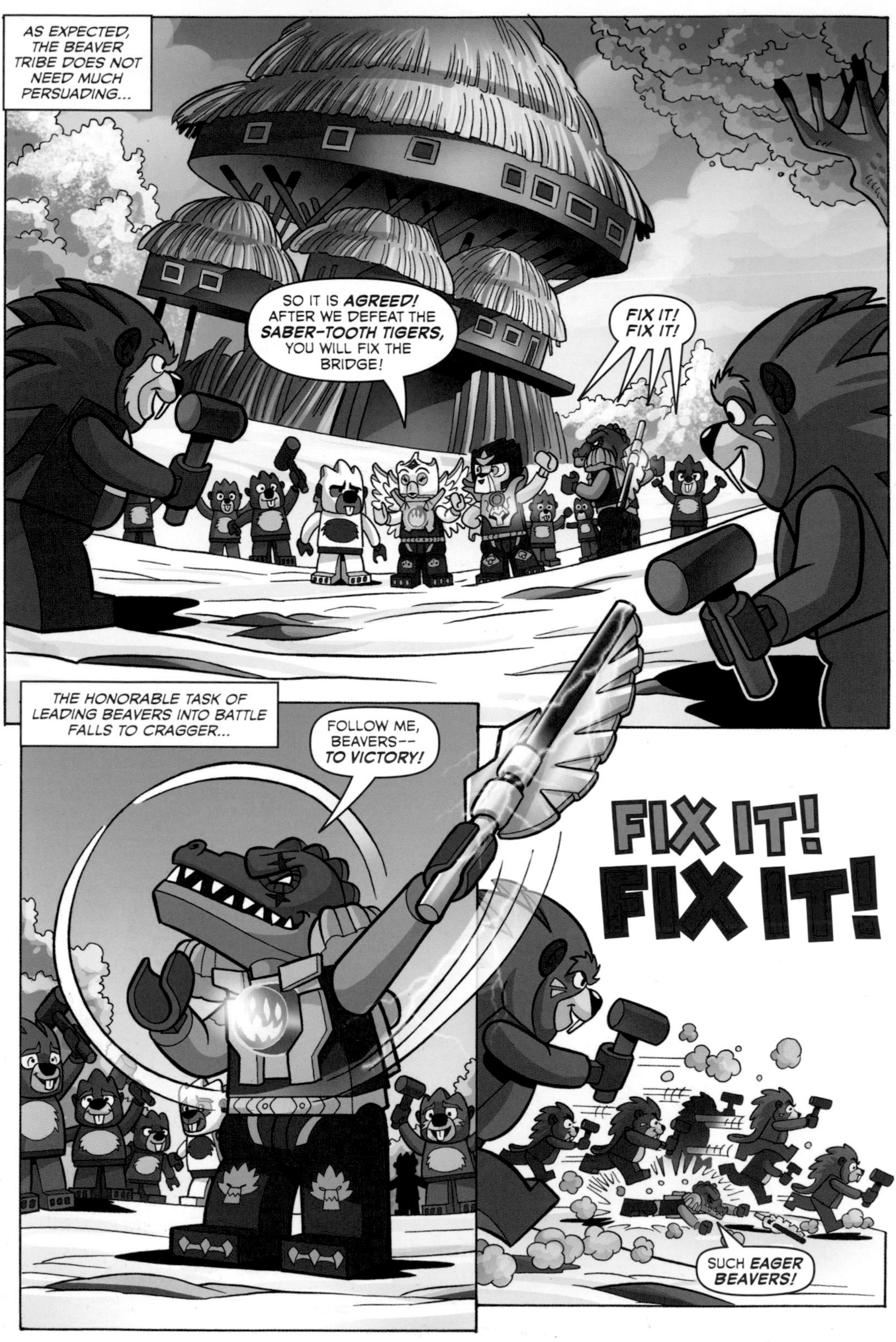
AS EXPECTED, THE BEAVER TRIBE DOES NOT NEED MUCH PERSUADING...
SO IT IS AGREED! AFTER WE DEFEAT THE SABER-TOOTH TIGERS, YOU WILL FIX THE BRIDGE!
FIX IT! FIX IT!
THE HONORABLE TASK OF LEADING BEAVERS INTO BATTLE FALLS TO CRAGGER...
FOLLOW ME, BEAVERS-- TO VICTORY!
FIX IT! FIX IT!
SUCH EAGER BEAVERS!

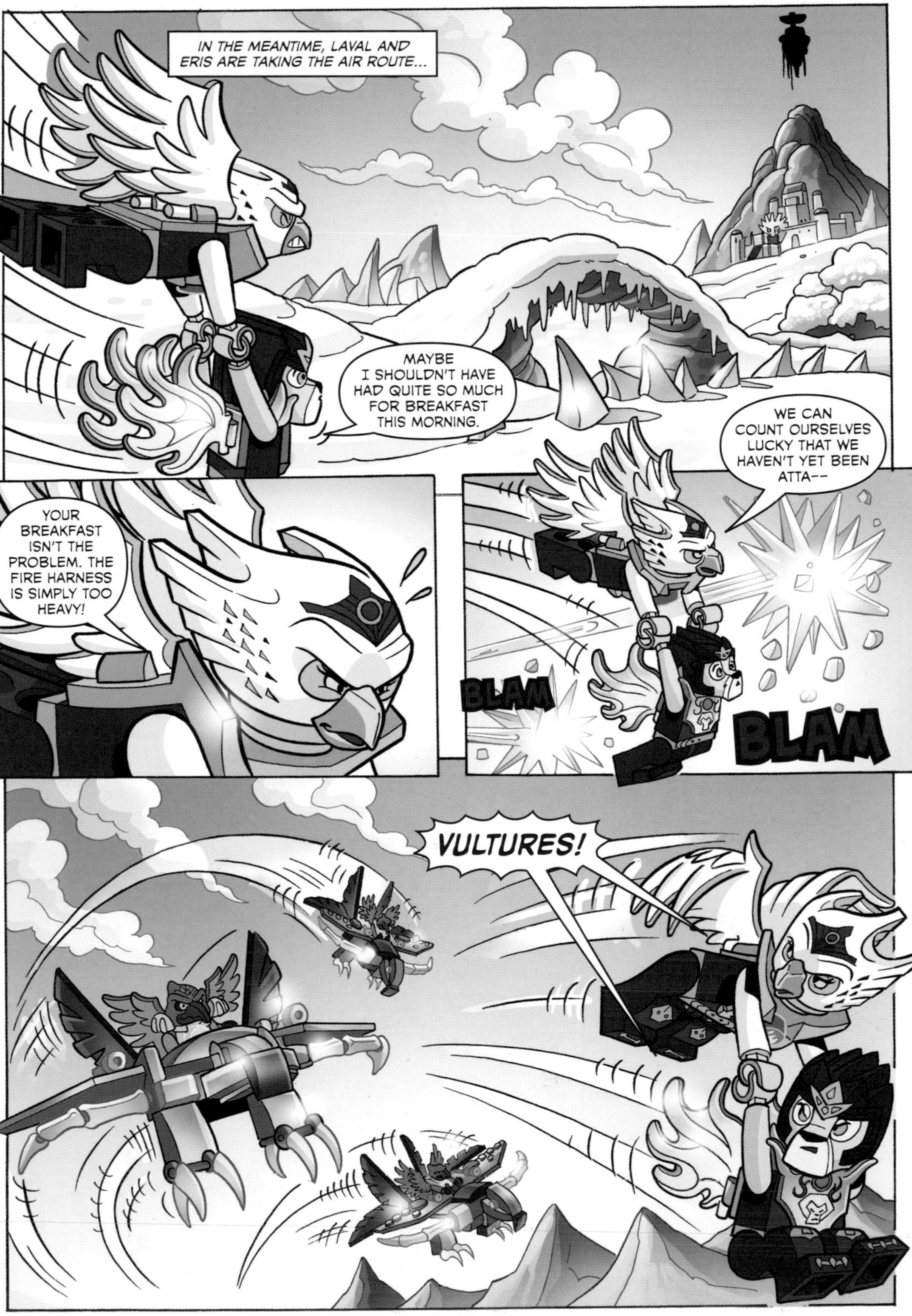

IN THE MEANTIME, LAVAL AND ERIS ARE TAKING THE AIR ROUTE...
MAYBE I SHOULDN'T HAVE HAD QUITE SO MUCH FOR BREAKFAST THIS MORNING.
YOUR BREAKFAST ISN'T THE PROBLEM. THE FIRE HARNESS IS SIMPLY TOO HEAVY!
WE CAN COUNT OURSELVES LUCKY THAT WE HAVEN'T YET BEEN ATTA--
BLAM
BLAM
VULTURES!

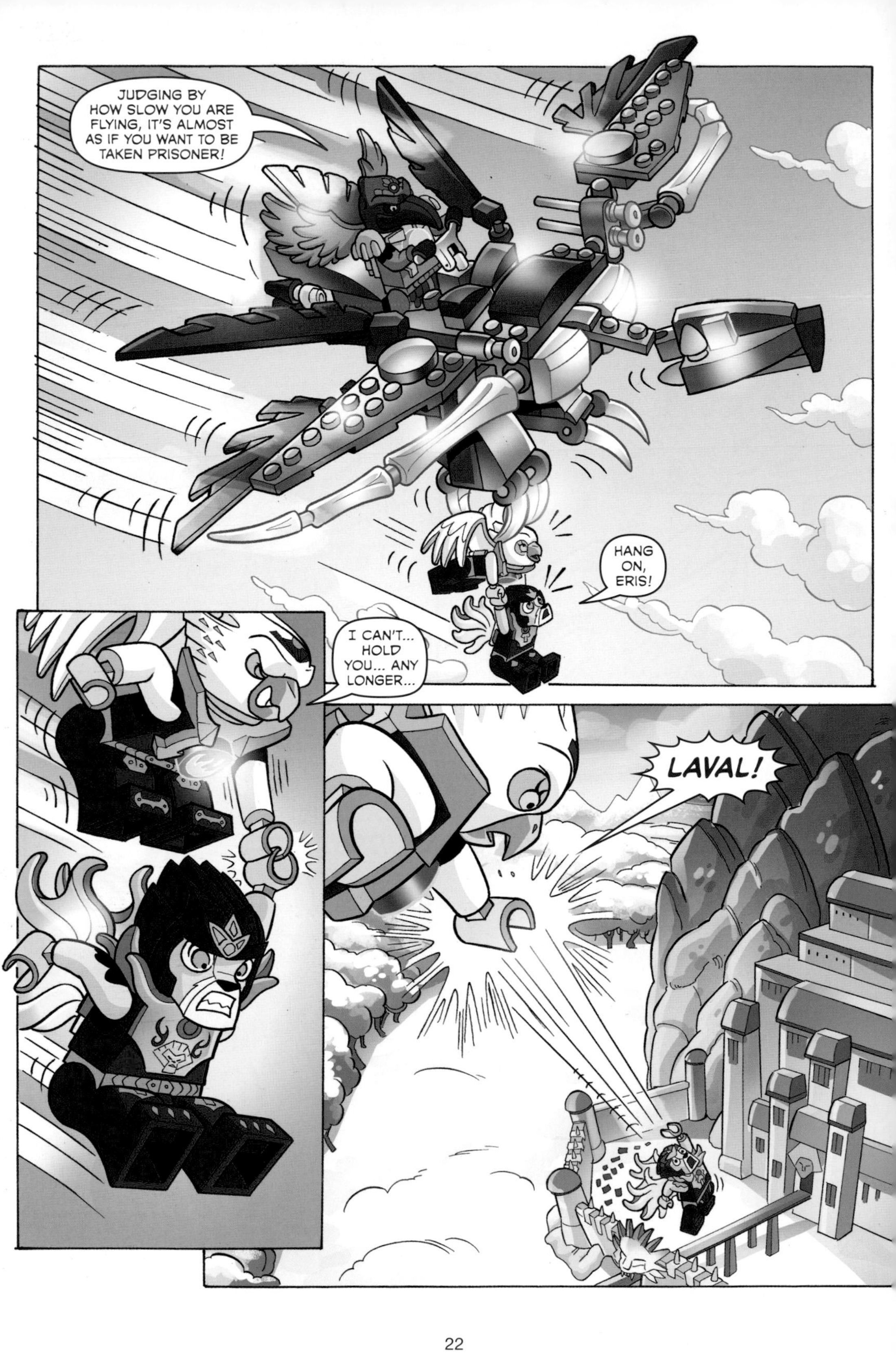

JUDGING BY HOW SLOW YOU ARE FLYING, IT'S ALMOST AS IF YOU WANT TO BE TAKEN PRISONER!
HANG ON, ERIS!
I CAN'T... HOLD YOU... ANY LONGER...
LAVAL!

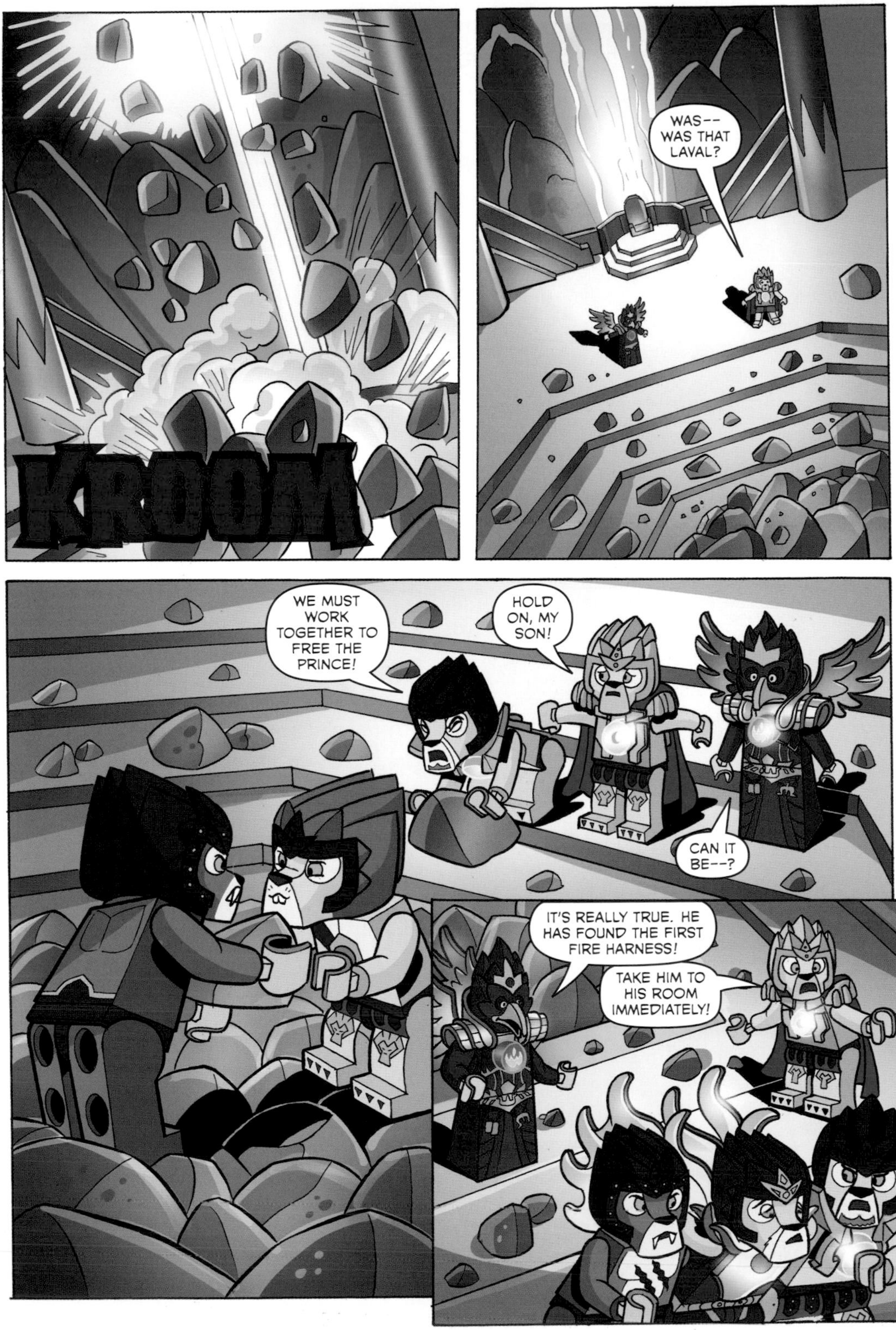
KROOM
WAS-- WAS THAT LAVAL?
WE MUST WORK TOGETHER TO FREE THE PRINCE!
HOLD ON, MY SON!
CAN IT BE--?
IT'S REALLY TRUE. HE HAS FOUND THE FIRST FIRE HARNESS!
TAKE HIM TO HIS ROOM IMMEDIATELY!

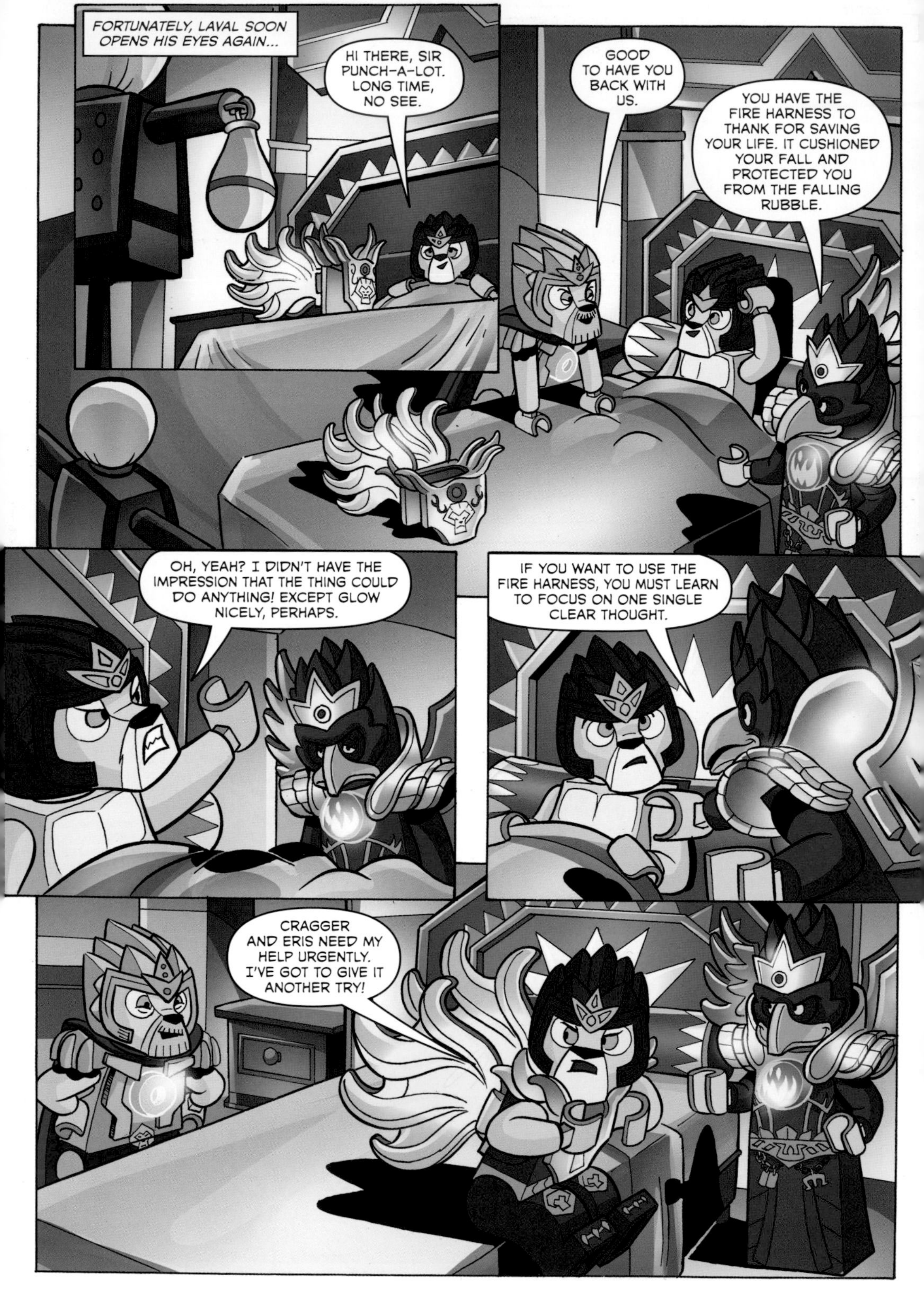
FORTUNATELY, LAVAL SOON OPENS HIS EYES AGAIN...
HI THERE, SIR PUNCH-A-LOT. LONG TIME, NO SEE.
GOOD TO HAVE YOU BACK WITH US.
YOU HAVE THE FIRE HARNESS TO THANK FOR SAVING YOUR LIFE. IT CUSHIONED YOUR FALL AND PROTECTED YOU FROM THE FALLING RUBBLE.
OH, YEAH? I DIDN'T HAVE THE IMPRESSION THAT THE THING COULD DO ANYTHING! EXCEPT GLOW NICELY, PERHAPS.
IF YOU WANT TO USE THE FIRE HARNESS, YOU MUST LEARN TO FOCUS ON ONE SINGLE CLEAR THOUGHT.
CRAGGER AND ERIS NEED MY HELP URGENTLY. I'VE GOT TO GIVE IT ANOTHER TRY!

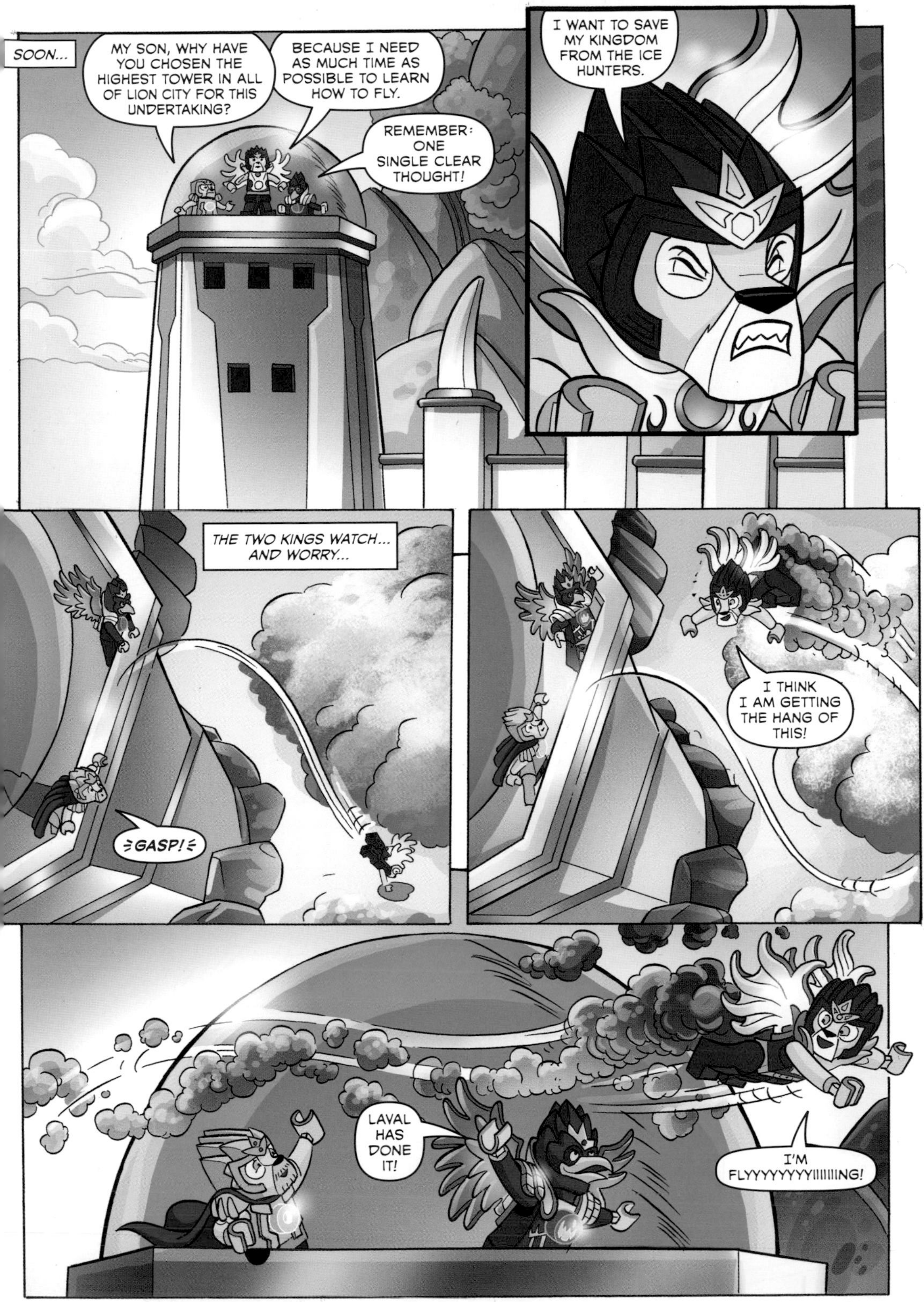
SOON...
MY SON, WHY HAVE YOU CHOSEN THE HIGHEST TOWER IN ALL OF LION CITY FOR THIS UNDERTAKING?
BECAUSE I NEED AS MUCH TIME AS POSSIBLE TO LEARN HOW TO FLY.
REMEMBER: ONE SINGLE CLEAR THOUGHT!
I WANT TO SAVE MY KINGDOM FROM THE ICE HUNTERS.
THE TWO KINGS WATCH... AND WORRY...
GASP!
I THINK I AM GETTING THE HANG OF THIS!
LAVAL HAS DONE IT!
I'M FLYYYYYYYYIIIIIIING!

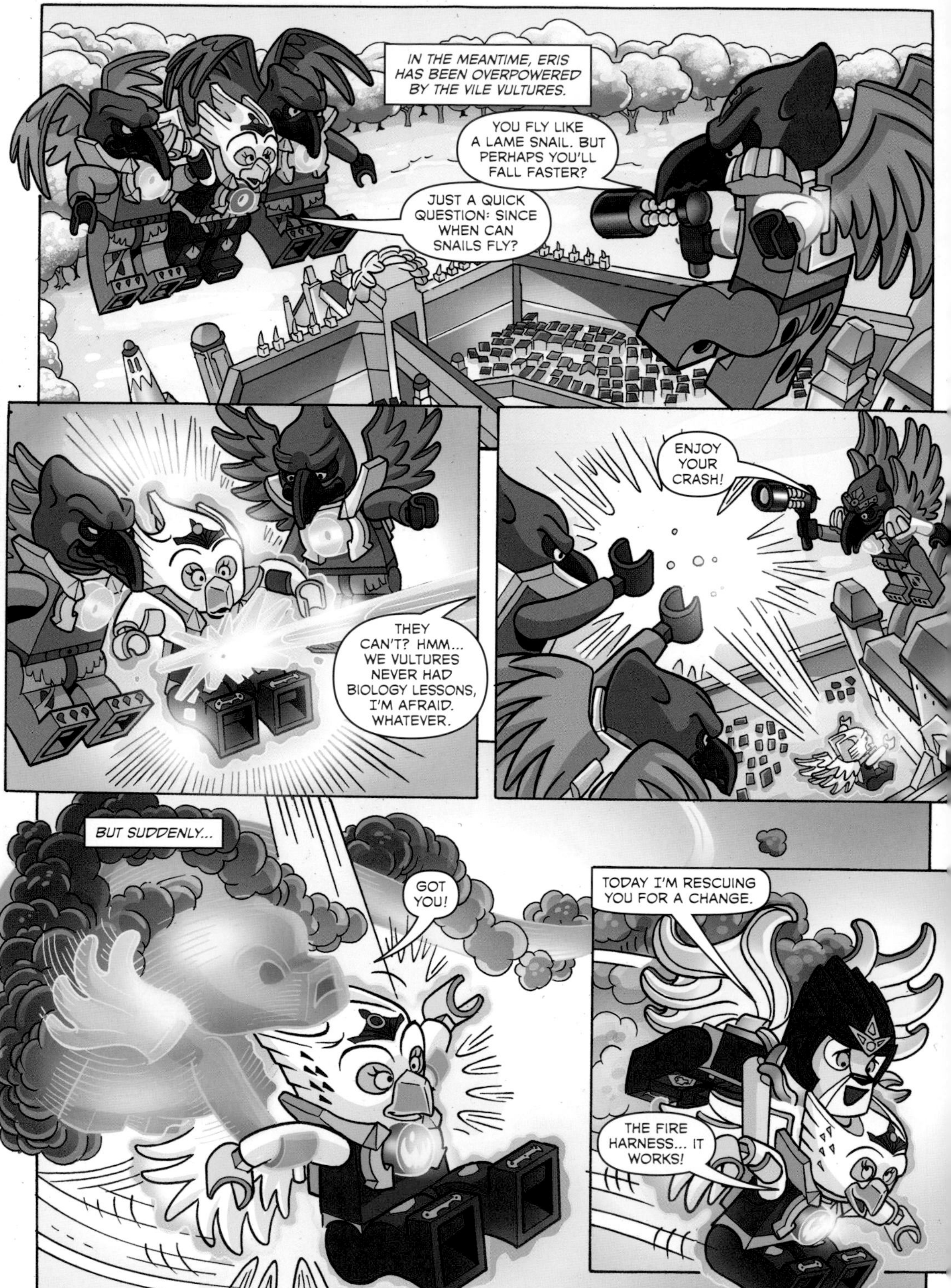
IN THE MEANTIME, ERIS HAS BEEN OVERPOWERED BY THE VILE VULTURES.
YOU FLY LIKE A LAME SNAIL. BUT PERHAPS YOU'LL FALL FASTER?
JUST A QUICK QUESTION: SINCE WHEN CAN SNAILS FLY?
THEY CAN'T? HMM... WE VULTURES NEVER HAD BIOLOGY LESSONS, I'M AFRAID. WHATEVER.
ENJOY YOUR CRASH!
BUT SUDDENLY...
GOT YOU!
TODAY I'M RESCUING YOU FOR A CHANGE.
THE FIRE HARNESS... IT WORKS!

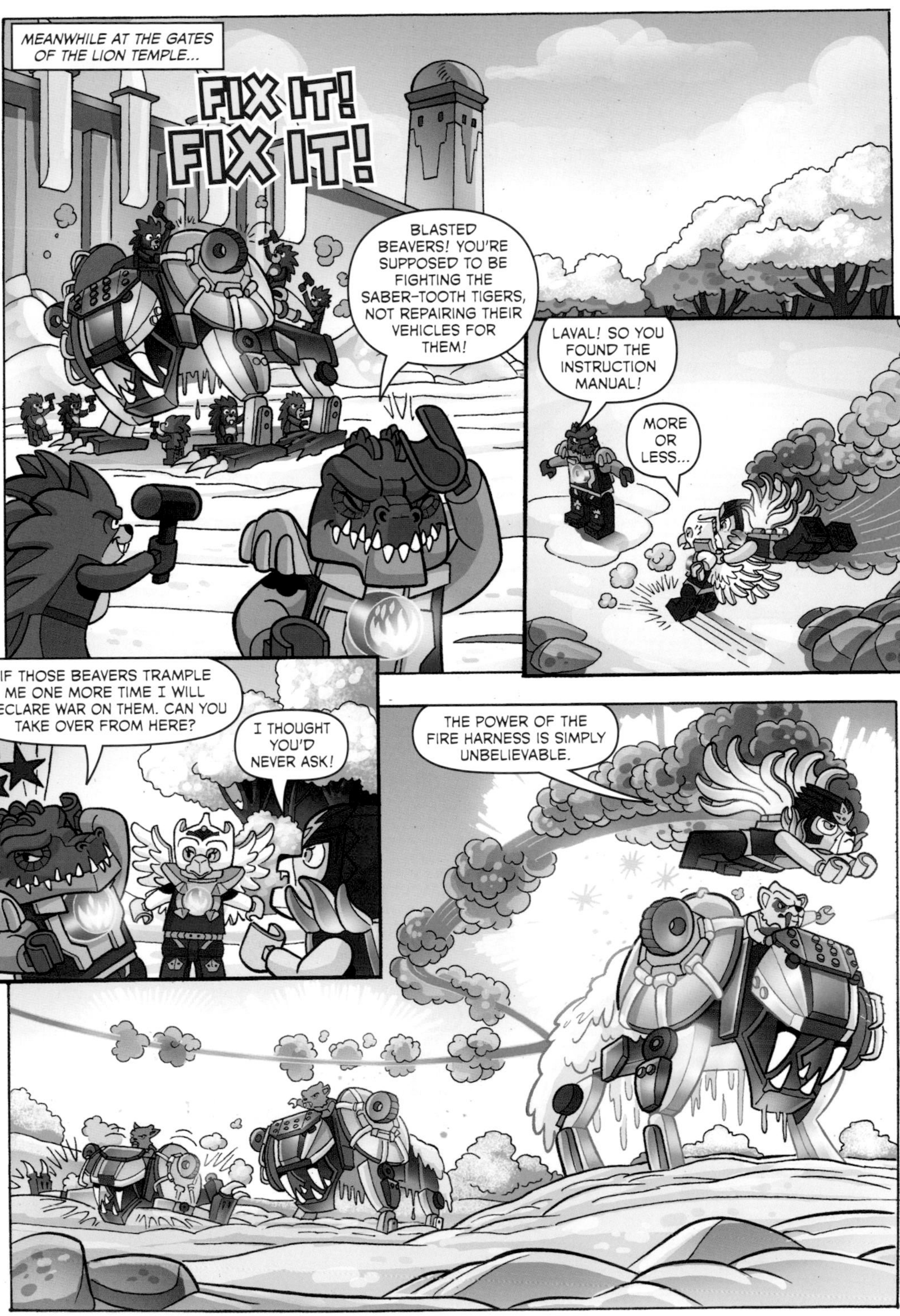
MEANWHILE AT THE GATES OF THE LION TEMPLE...
FIX IT! FIX IT!
BLASTED BEAVERS! YOU'RE SUPPOSED TO BE FIGHTING THE SABER-TOOTH TIGERS, NOT REPAIRING THEIR VEHICLES FOR THEM!
LAVAL! SO YOU FOUND THE INSTRUCTION MANUAL!
MORE OR LESS...
IF THOSE BEAVERS TRAMPLE ME ONE MORE TIME I WILL DECLARE WAR ON THEM. CAN YOU TAKE OVER FROM HERE?
I THOUGHT YOU'D NEVER ASK!
THE POWER OF THE FIRE HARNESS IS SIMPLY UNBELIEVABLE.

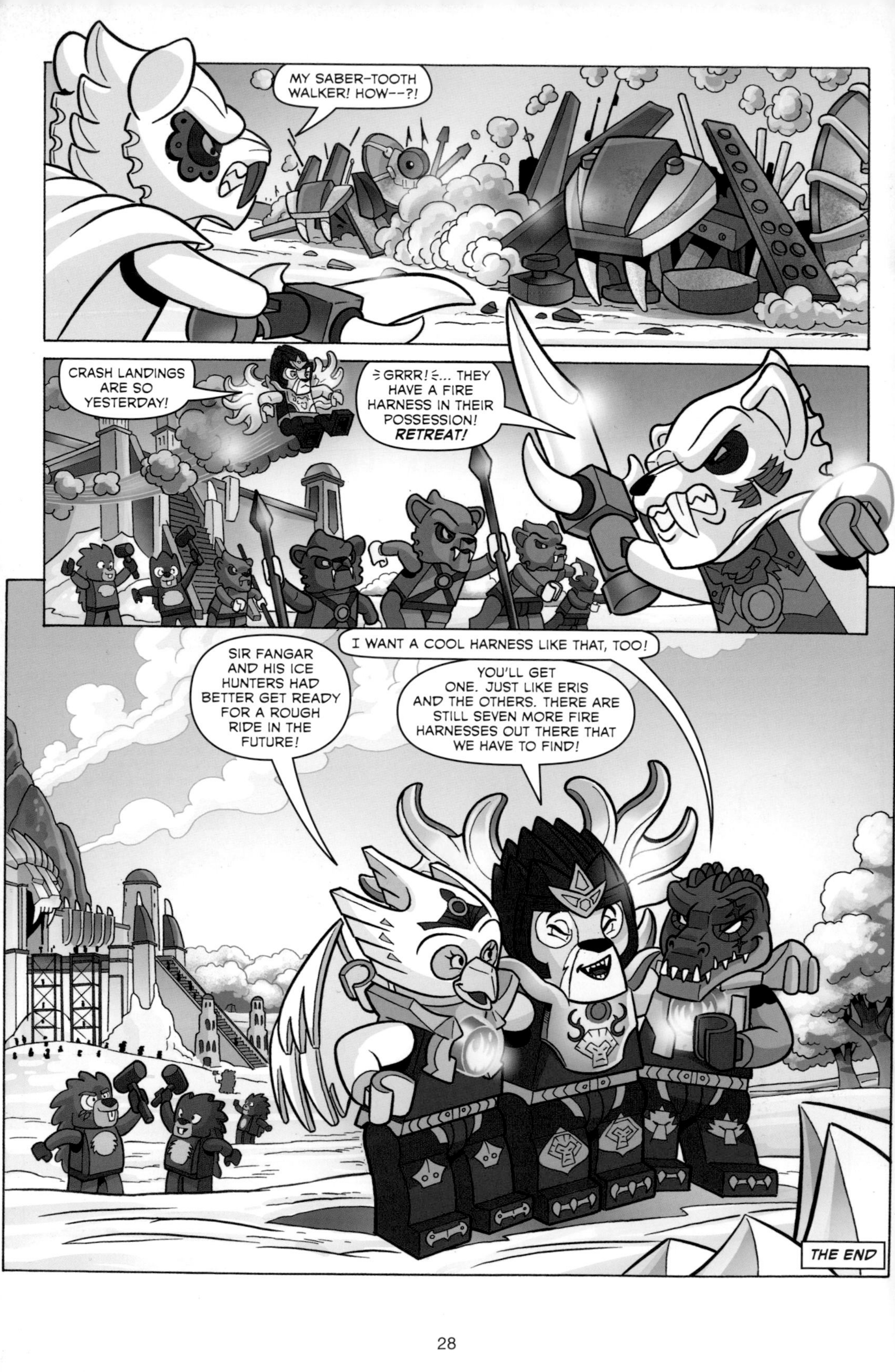
MY SABER-TOOTH WALKER! HOW--?!
CRASH LANDINGS ARE SO YESTERDAY!
GRRR!... THEY HAVE A FIRE HARNESS IN THEIR POSSESSION! RETREAT!
SIR FANGAR AND HIS ICE HUNTERS HAD BETTER GET READY FOR A ROUGH RIDE IN THE FUTURE!
I WANT A COOL HARNESS LIKE THAT, TOO!
YOU'LL GET ONE. JUST LIKE ERIS AND THE OTHERS. THERE ARE STILL SEVEN MORE FIRE HARNESSES OUT THERE THAT WE HAVE TO FIND!
THE END

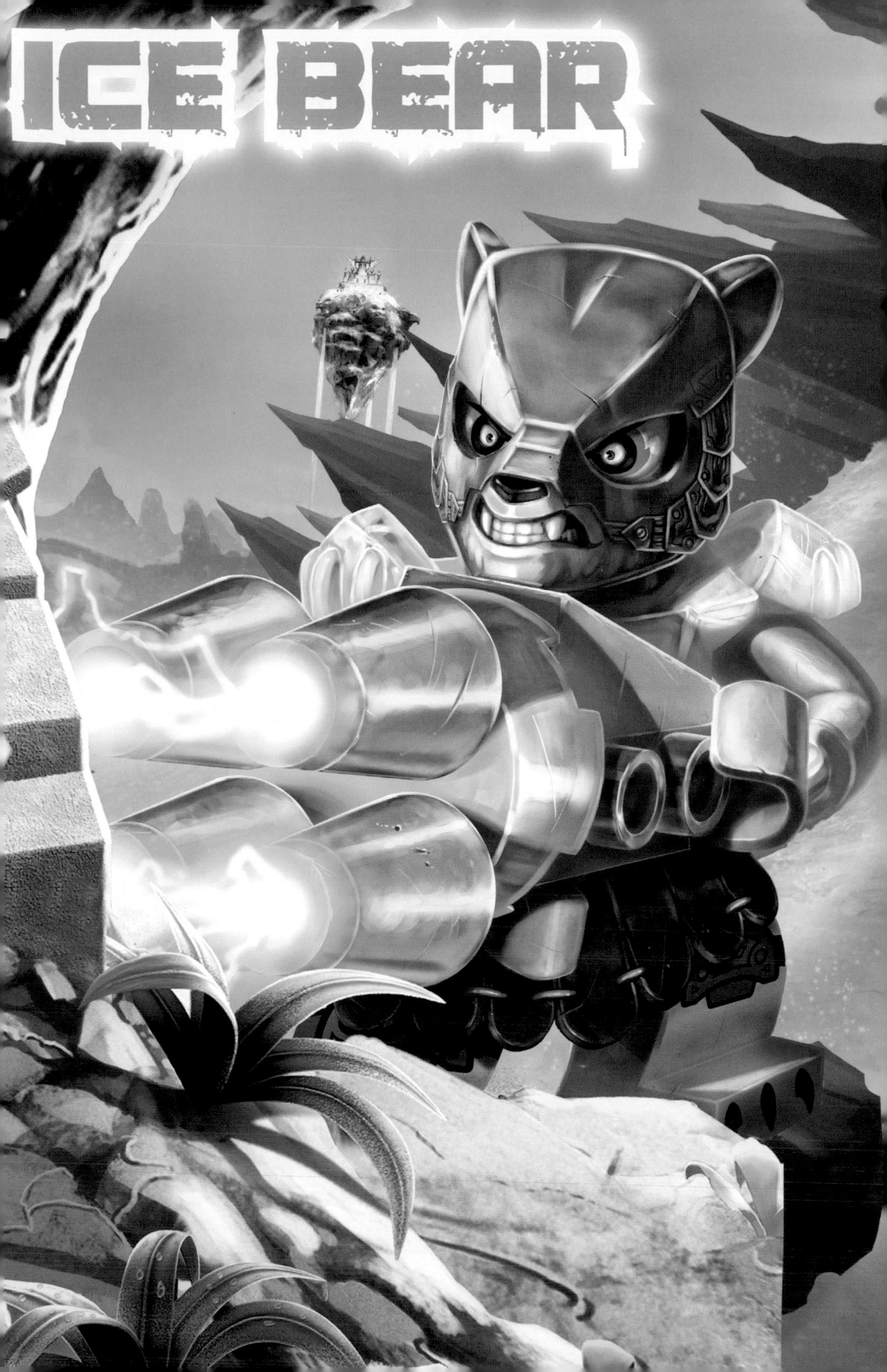
ICE BEAR

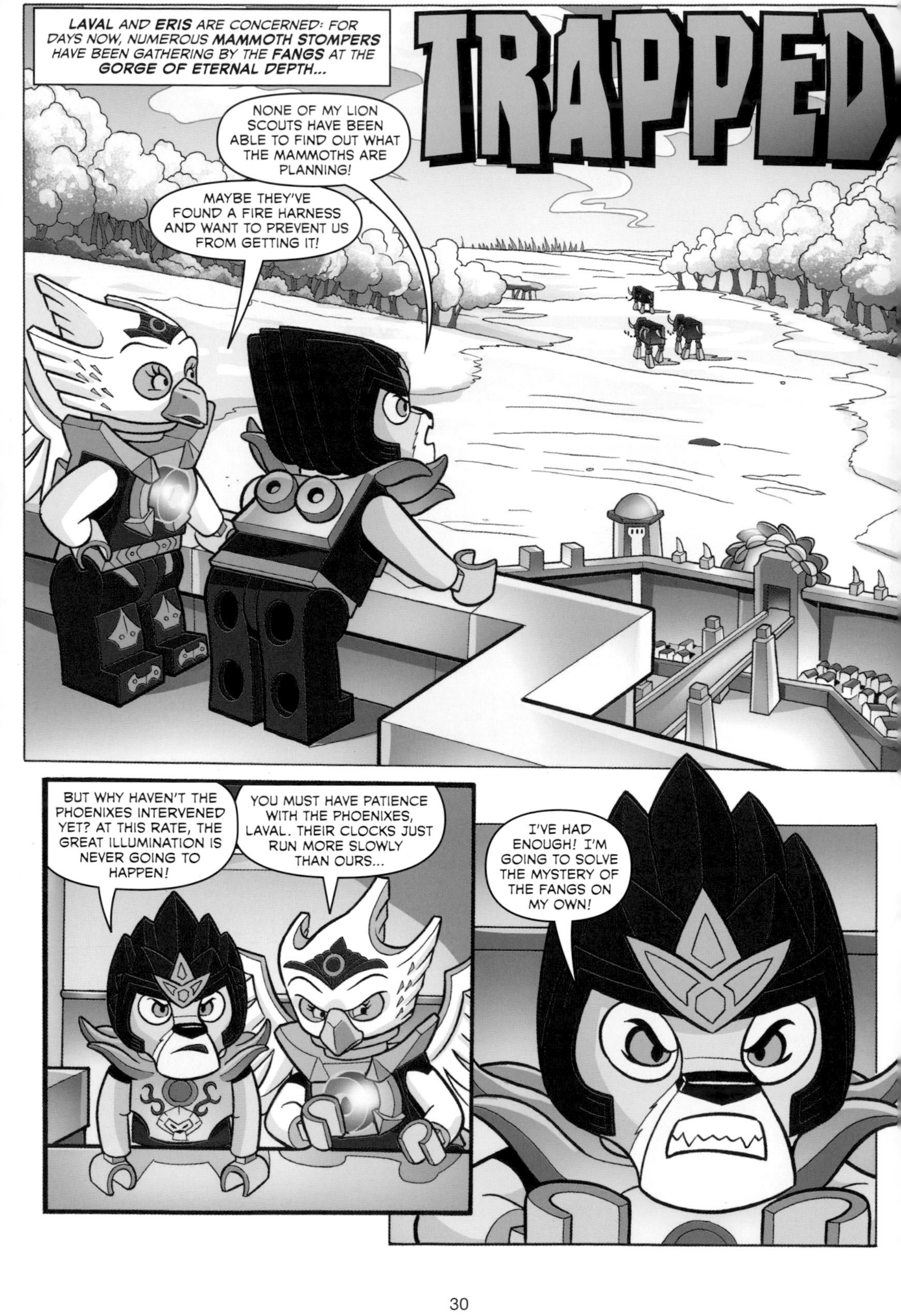
LAVAL AND ERIS ARE CONCERNED: FOR DAYS NOW, NUMEROUS MAMMOTH STOMPERS HAVE BEEN GATHERING BY THE FANGS AT THE GORGE OF ETERNAL DEPTH...
TRAPPED
NONE OF MY LION SCOUTS HAVE BEEN ABLE TO FIND OUT WHAT THE MAMMOTHS ARE PLANNING!
MAYBE THEY'VE FOUND A FIRE HARNESS AND WANT TO PREVENT US FROM GETTING IT!
BUT WHY HAVEN'T THE PHOENIXES INTERVENED YET? AT THIS RATE, THE GREAT ILLUMINATION IS NEVER GOING TO HAPPEN!
YOU MUST HAVE PATIENCE WITH THE PHOENIXES, LAVAL. THEIR CLOCKS JUST RUN MORE SLOWLY THAN OURS...
I'VE HAD ENOUGH! I'M GOING TO SOLVE THE MYSTERY OF THE FANGS ON MY OWN!

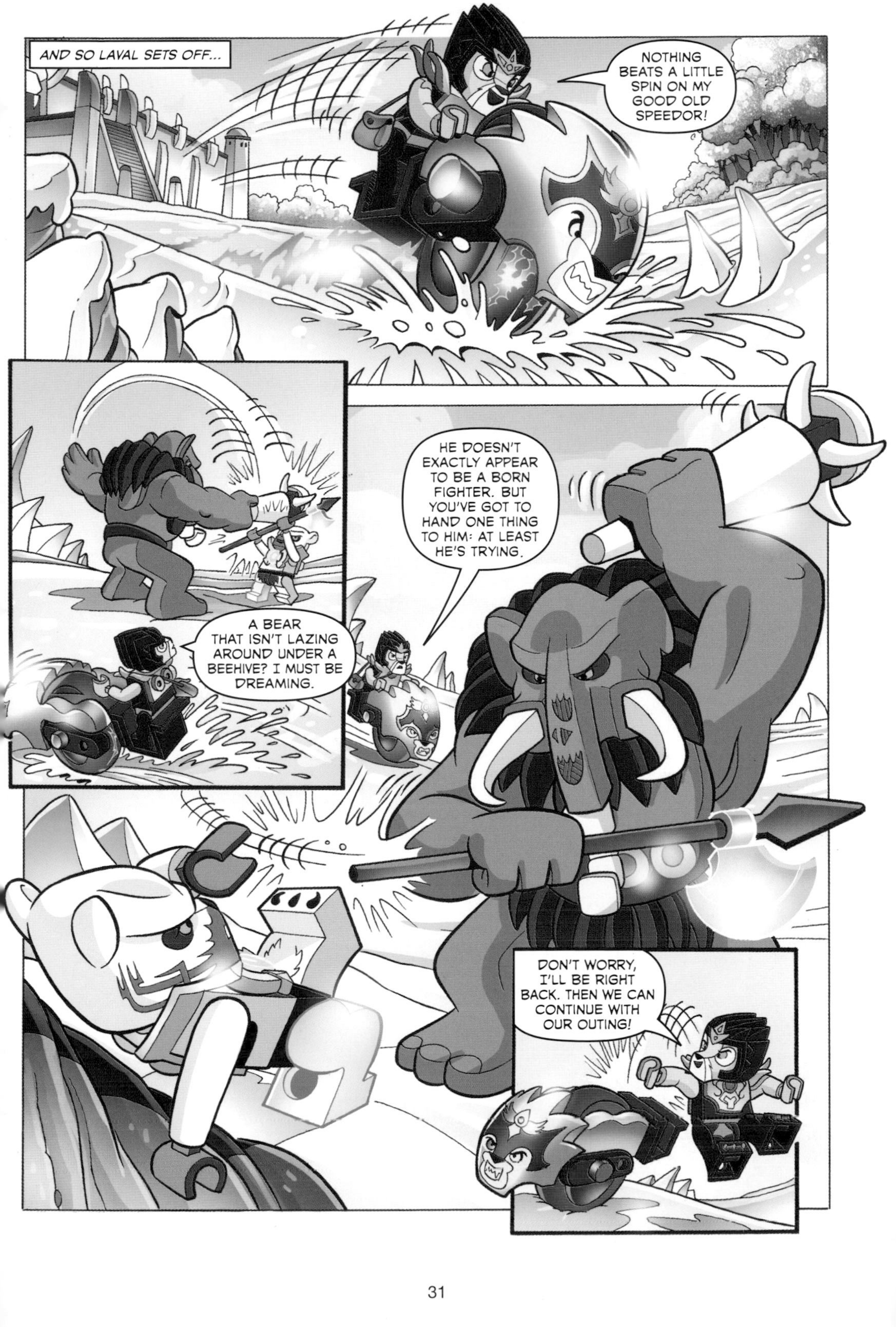
AND SO LAVAL SETS OFF...
NOTHING BEATS A LITTLE SPIN ON MY GOOD OLD SPEEDOR!
A BEAR THAT ISN'T LAZING AROUND UNDER A BEEHIVE? I MUST BE DREAMING.
HE DOESN'T EXACTLY APPEAR TO BE A BORN FIGHTER. BUT YOU'VE GOT TO HAND ONE THING TO HIM: AT LEAST HE'S TRYING.
DON'T WORRY, I'LL BE RIGHT BACK. THEN WE CAN CONTINUE WITH OUR OUTING!

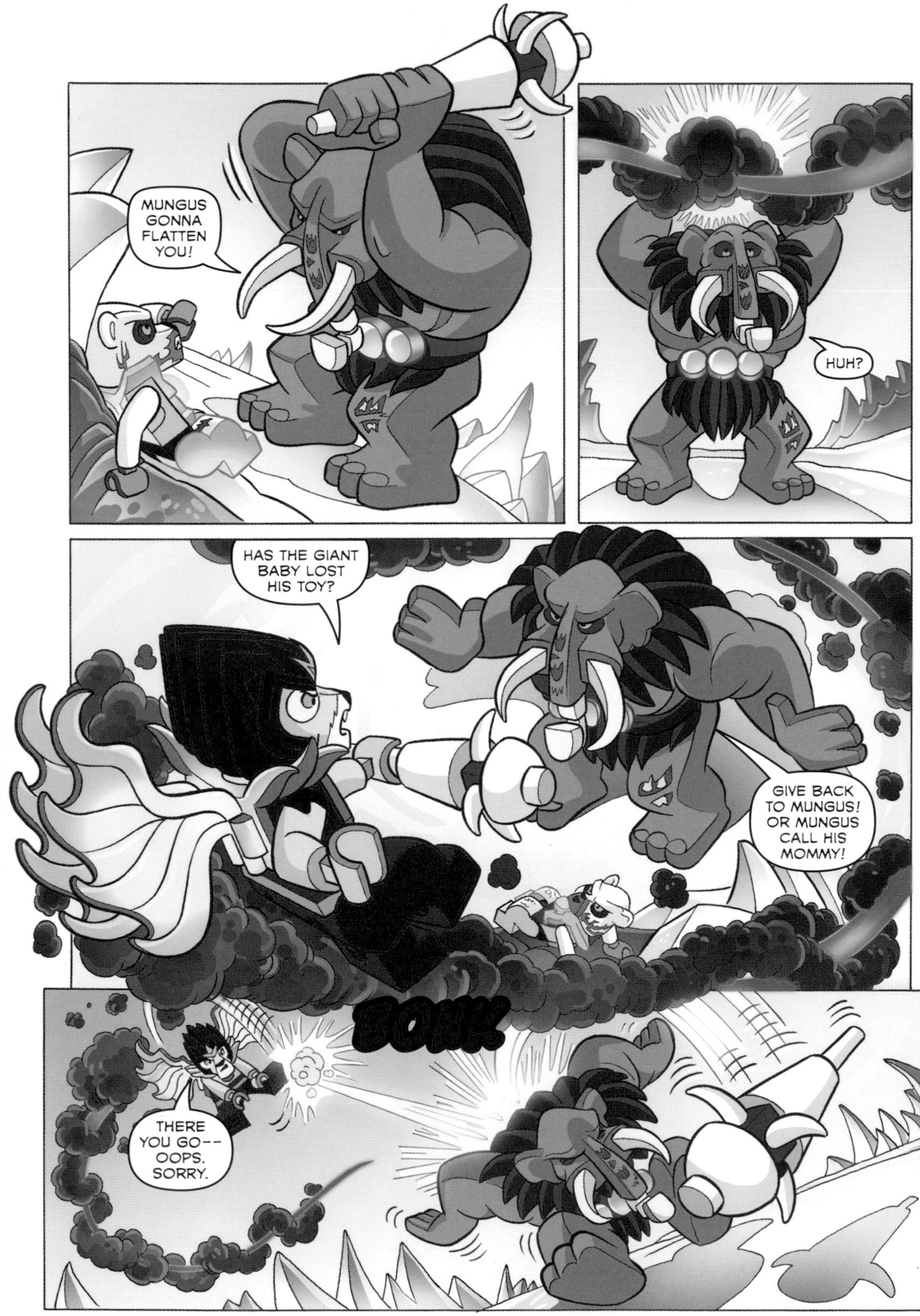
MUNGUS GONNA FLATTEN YOU!
HUH?
HAS THE GIANT BABY LOST HIS TOY?
GIVE BACK TO MUNGUS! OR MUNGUS CALL HIS MOMMY!
BONK!
THERE YOU GO-- OOPS. SORRY.

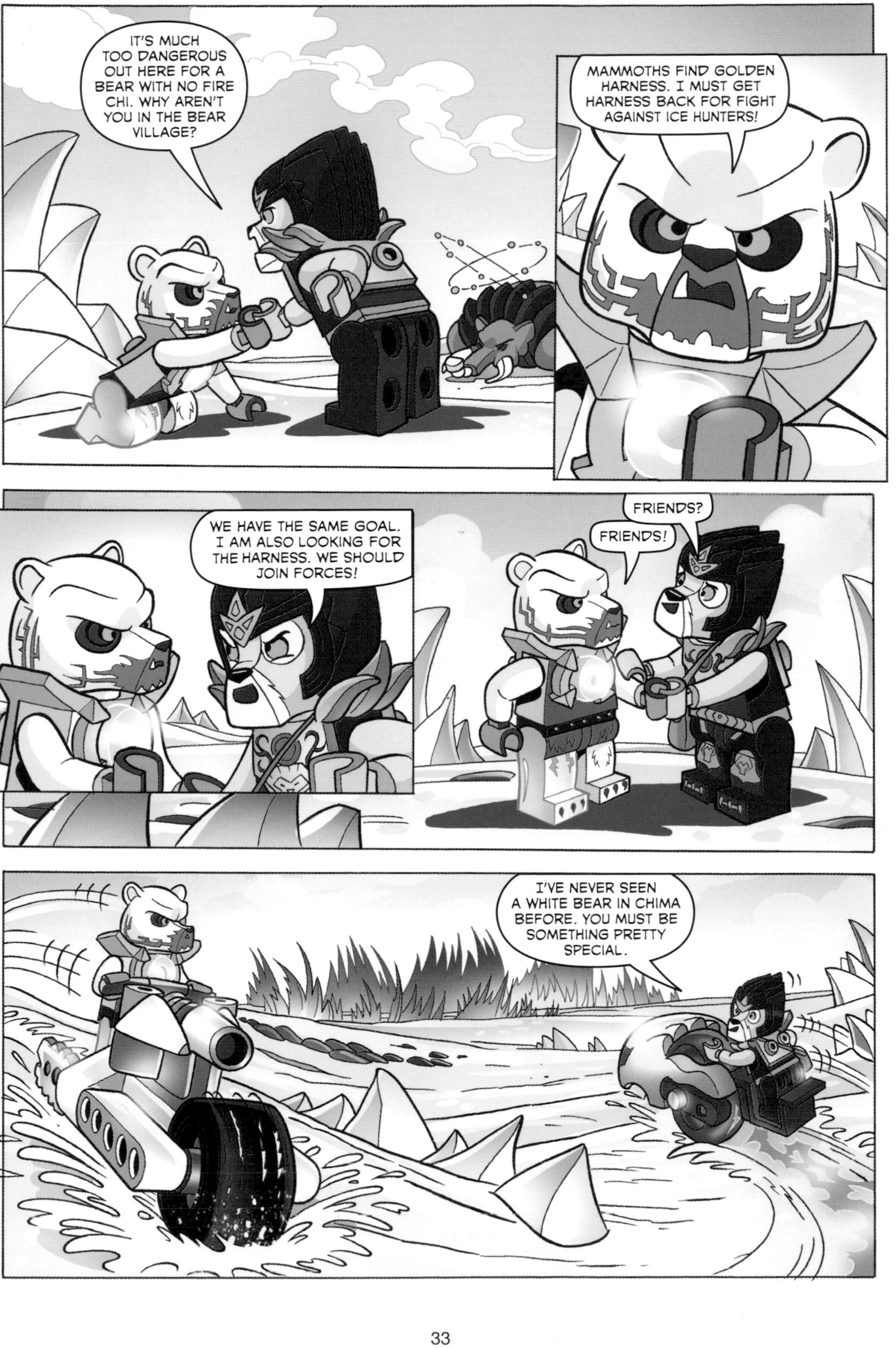
IT'S MUCH TOO DANGEROUS OUT HERE FOR A BEAR WITH NO FIRE CHI. WHY AREN'T YOU IN THE BEAR VILLAGE?
MAMMOTHS FIND GOLDEN HARNESS. I MUST GET HARNESS BACK FOR FIGHT AGAINST ICE HUNTERS!
WE HAVE THE SAME GOAL. I AM ALSO LOOKING FOR THE HARNESS. WE SHOULD JOIN FORCES!
FRIENDS?
FRIENDS!
I'VE NEVER SEEN A WHITE BEAR IN CHIMA BEFORE. YOU MUST BE SOMETHING PRETTY SPECIAL.

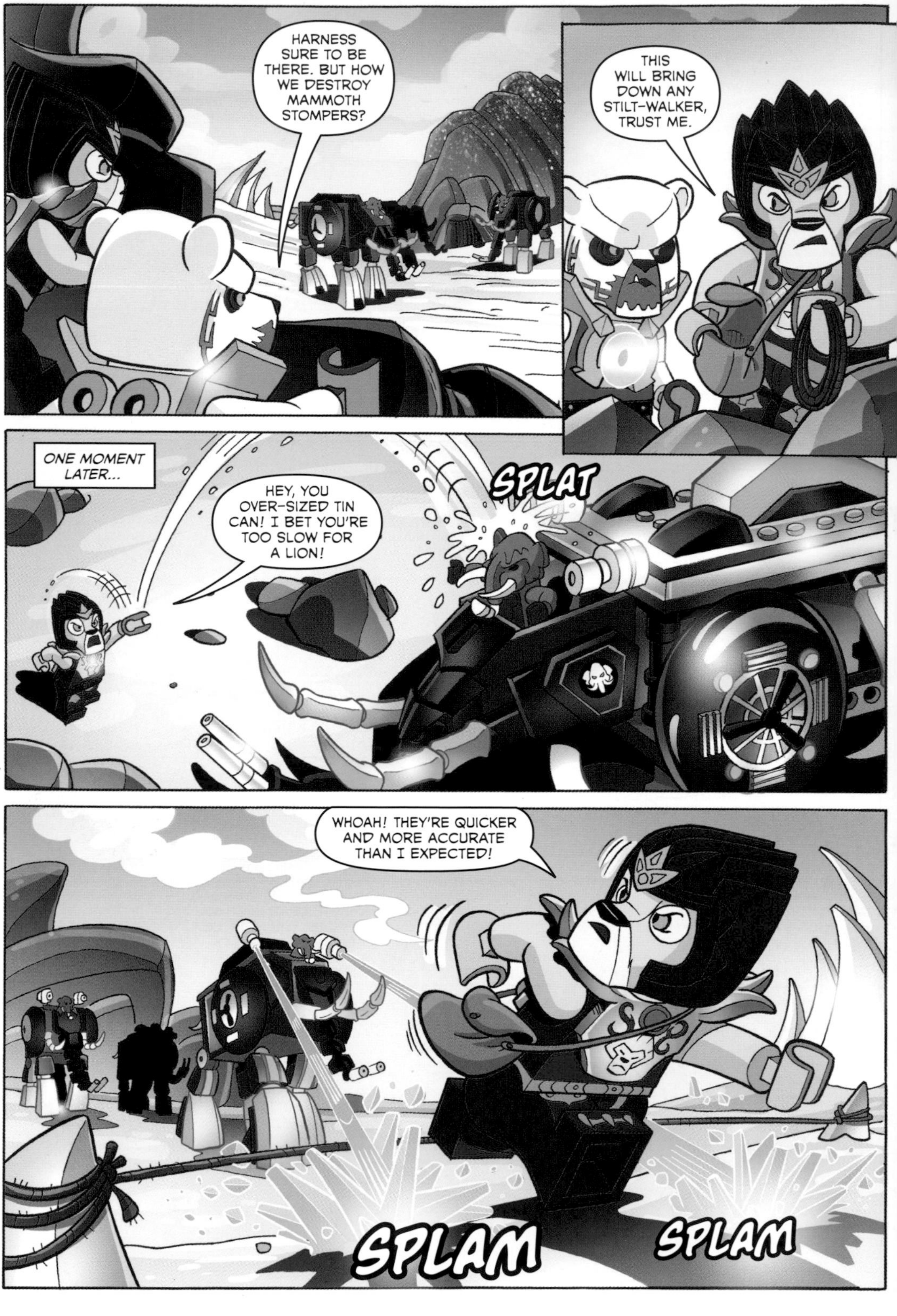
HARNESS SURE TO BE THERE. BUT HOW WE DESTROY MAMMOTH STOMPERS?
THIS WILL BRING DOWN ANY STILT-WALKER, TRUST ME.
ONE MOMENT LATER...
HEY, YOU OVER-SIZED TIN CAN! I BET YOU'RE TOO SLOW FOR A LION!
SPLAT
WHOAH! THEY'RE QUICKER AND MORE ACCURATE THAN I EXPECTED!
SPLAM
SPLAM

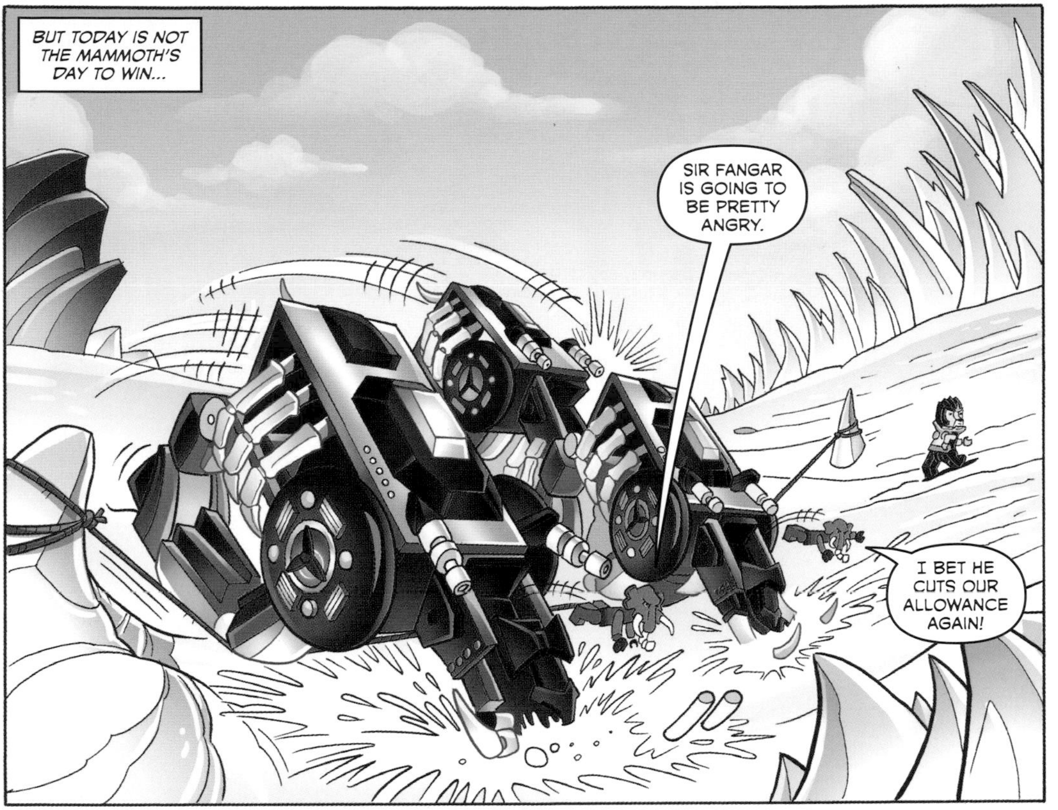
BUT TODAY IS NOT THE MAMMOTH'S DAY TO WIN...
SIR FANGAR IS GOING TO BE PRETTY ANGRY.
I BET HE CUTS OUR ALLOWANCE AGAIN!

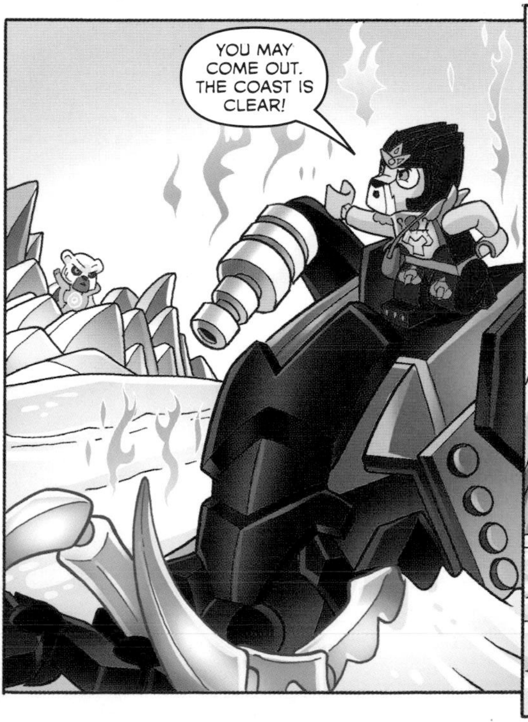
YOU MAY COME OUT. THE COAST IS CLEAR!

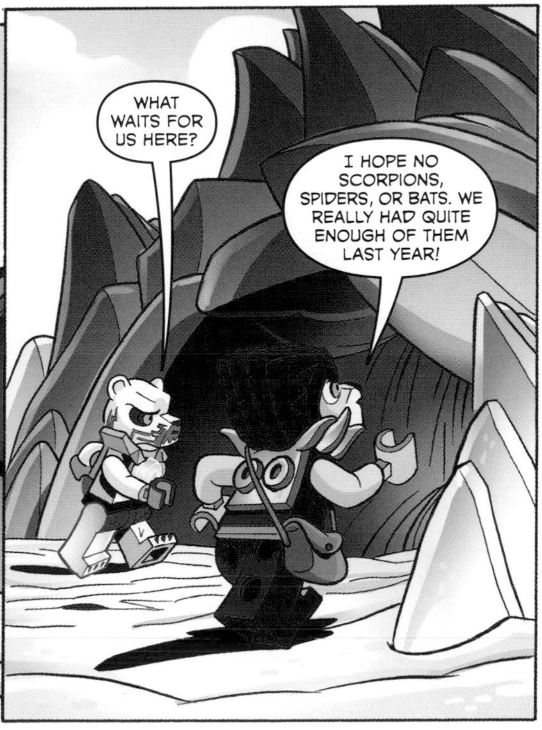
WHAT WAITS FOR US HERE?
I HOPE NO SCORPIONS, SPIDERS, OR BATS. WE REALLY HAD QUITE ENOUGH OF THEM LAST YEAR!

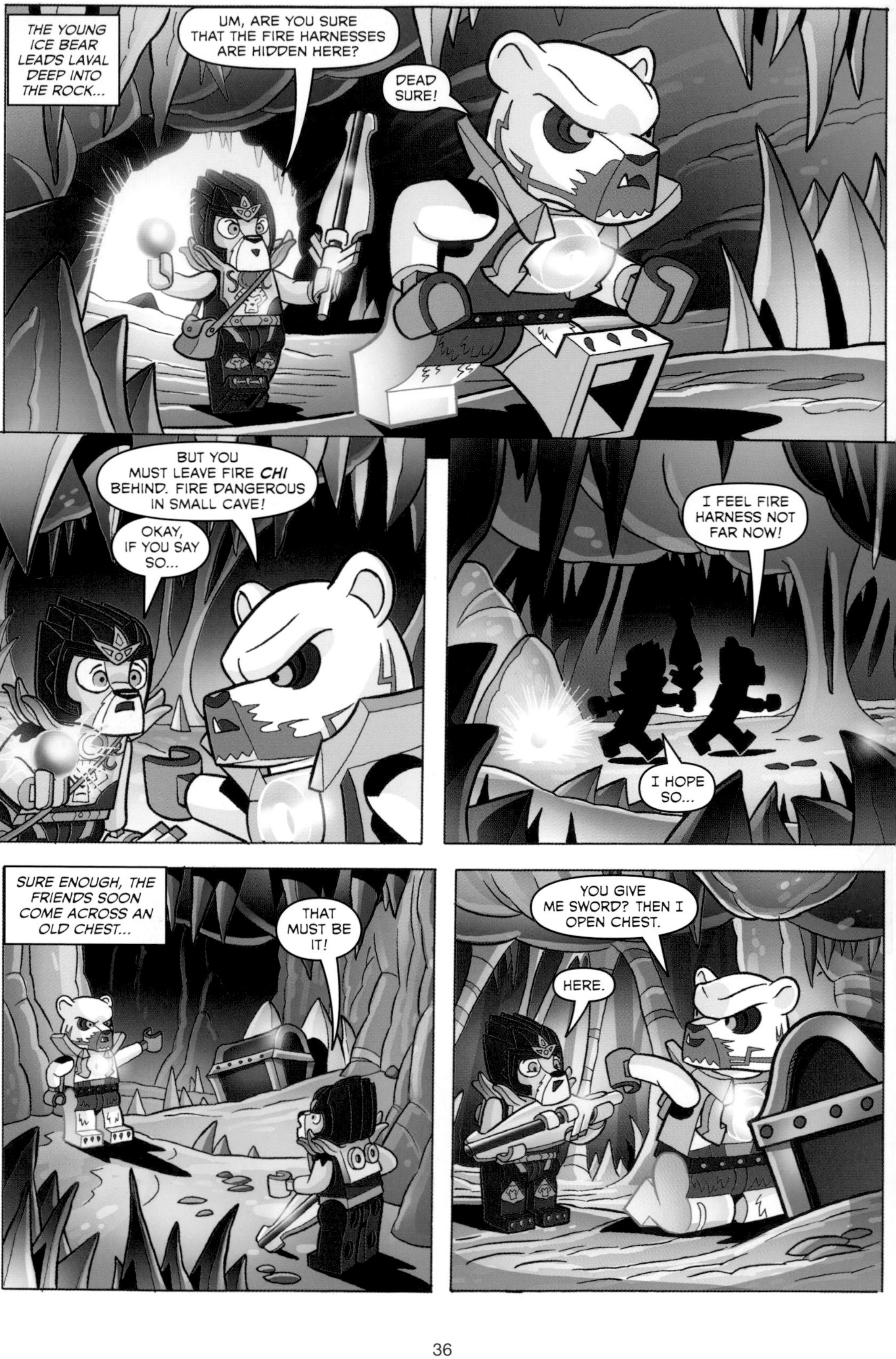
THE YOUNG ICE BEAR LEADS LAVAL DEEP INTO THE ROCK...
UM, ARE YOU SURE THAT THE FIRE HARNESSES ARE HIDDEN HERE?
DEAD SURE!
BUT YOU MUST LEAVE FIRE CHI BEHIND. FIRE DANGEROUS IN SMALL CAVE!
OKAY, IF YOU SAY SO...
I FEEL FIRE HARNESS NOT FAR NOW!
I HOPE SO...
SURE ENOUGH, THE FRIENDS SOON COME ACROSS AN OLD CHEST...
THAT MUST BE IT!
YOU GIVE ME SWORD? THEN I OPEN CHEST.
HERE.

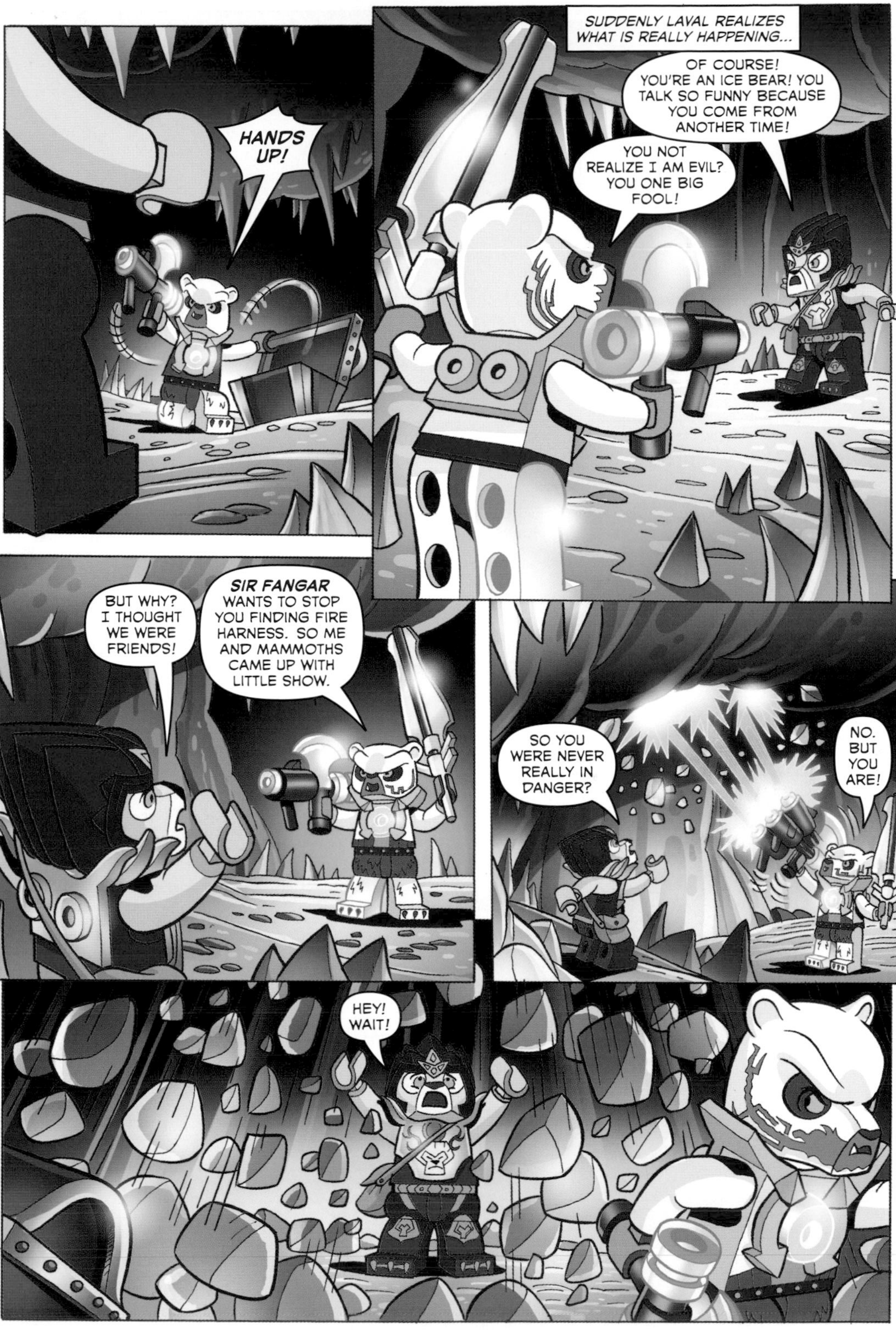
HANDS UP!
SUDDENLY LAVAL REALIZES WHAT IS REALLY HAPPENING...
OF COURSE! YOU'RE AN ICE BEAR! YOU TALK SO FUNNY BECAUSE YOU COME FROM ANOTHER TIME!
YOU NOT REALIZE I AM EVIL? YOU ONE BIG FOOL!
BUT WHY? I THOUGHT WE WERE FRIENDS!
SIR FANGAR WANTS TO STOP YOU FINDING FIRE HARNESS. SO ME AND MAMMOTHS CAME UP WITH LITTLE SHOW.
SO YOU WERE NEVER REALLY IN DANGER?
NO. BUT YOU ARE!
HEY! WAIT!

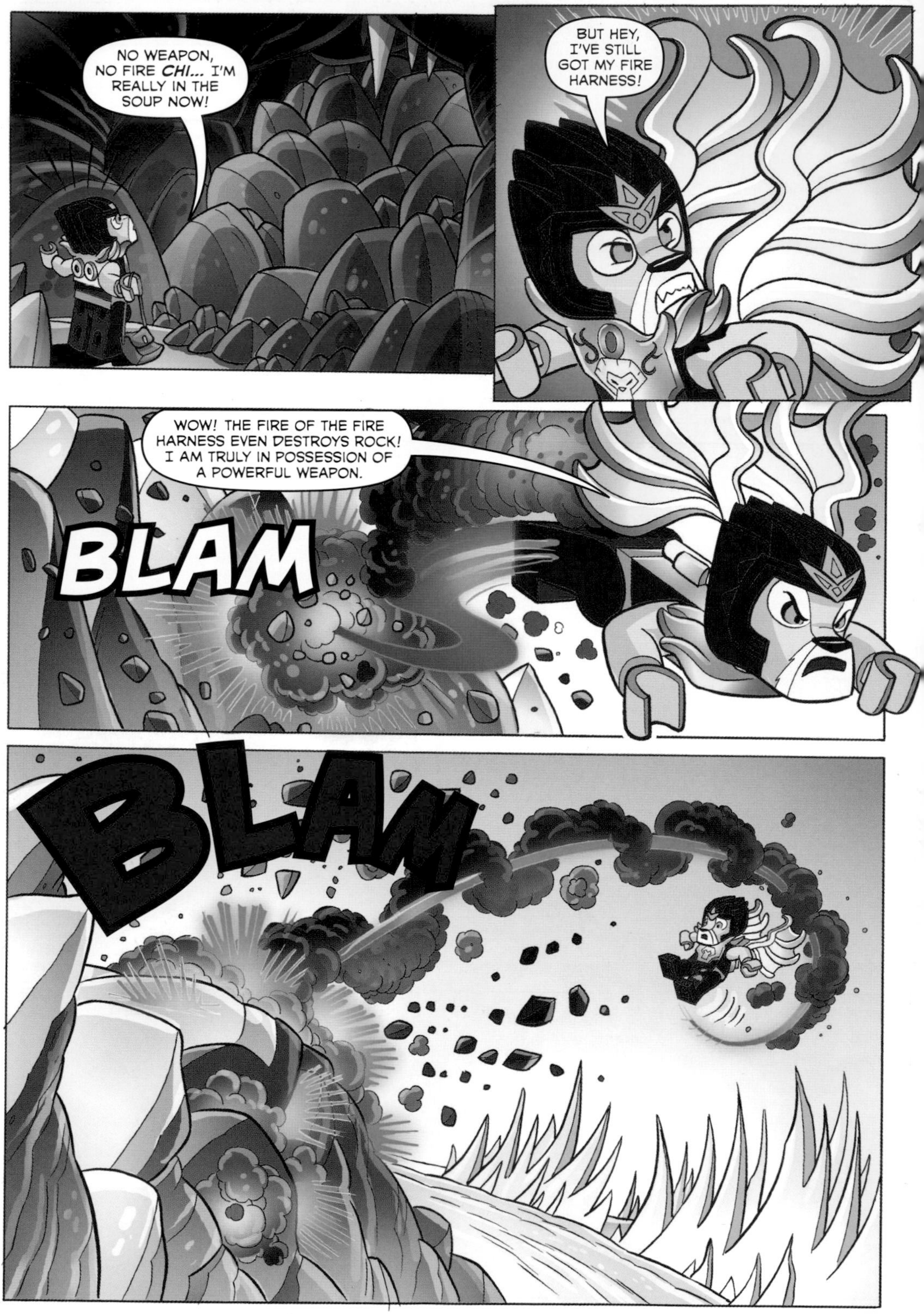
NO WEAPON, NO FIRE *CHI*... I'M REALLY IN THE SOUP NOW!
BUT HEY, I'VE STILL GOT MY FIRE HARNESS!
WOW! THE FIRE OF THE FIRE HARNESS EVEN DESTROYS ROCK! I AM TRULY IN POSSESSION OF A POWERFUL WEAPON.
BLAM
BLAM

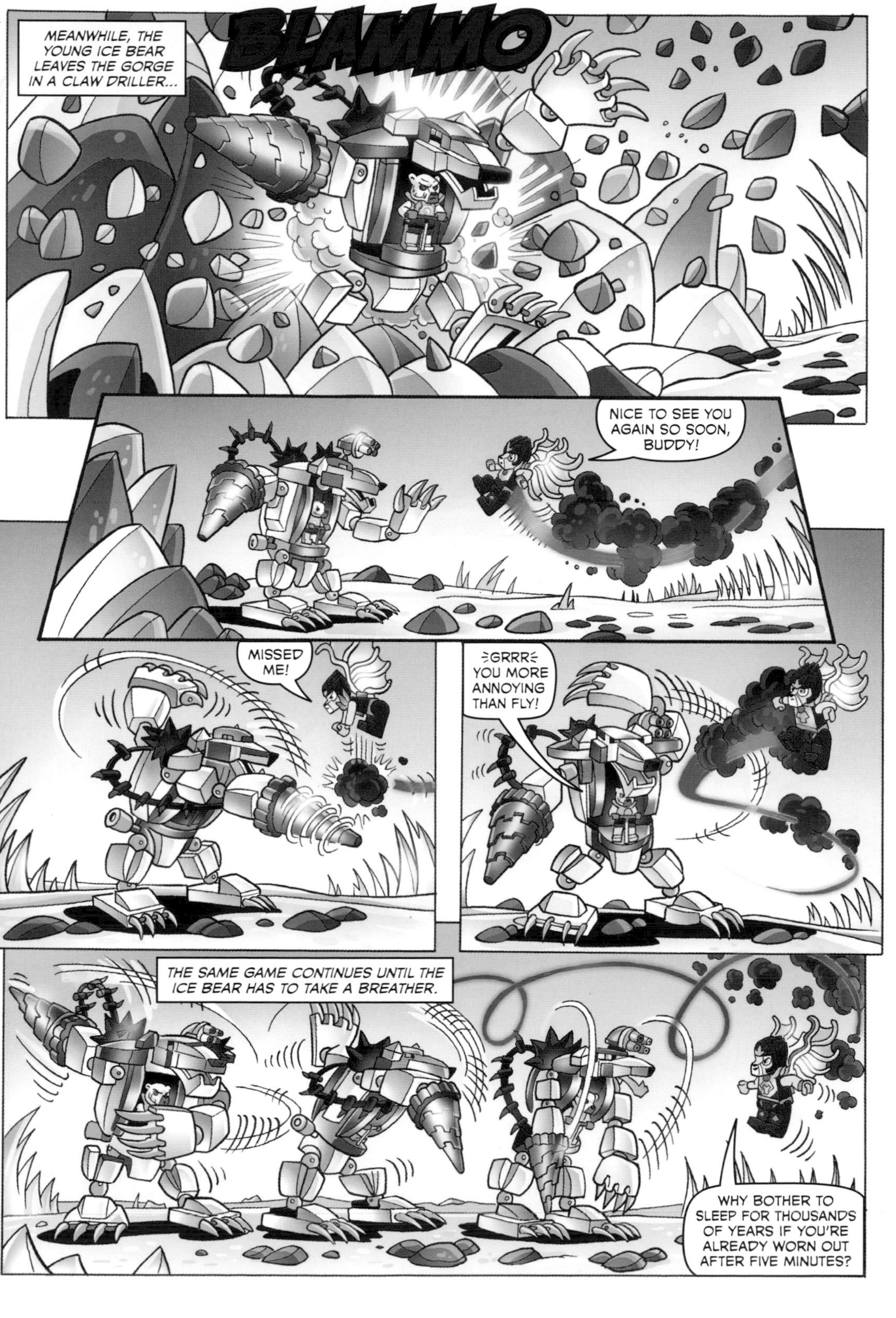

MEANWHILE, THE YOUNG ICE BEAR LEAVES THE GORGE IN A CLAW DRILLER...
BLAMMO
NICE TO SEE YOU AGAIN SO SOON, BUDDY!
MISSED ME!
GRRR YOU MORE ANNOYING THAN FLY!
THE SAME GAME CONTINUES UNTIL THE ICE BEAR HAS TO TAKE A BREATHER.
WHY BOTHER TO SLEEP FOR THOUSANDS OF YEARS IF YOU'RE ALREADY WORN OUT AFTER FIVE MINUTES?

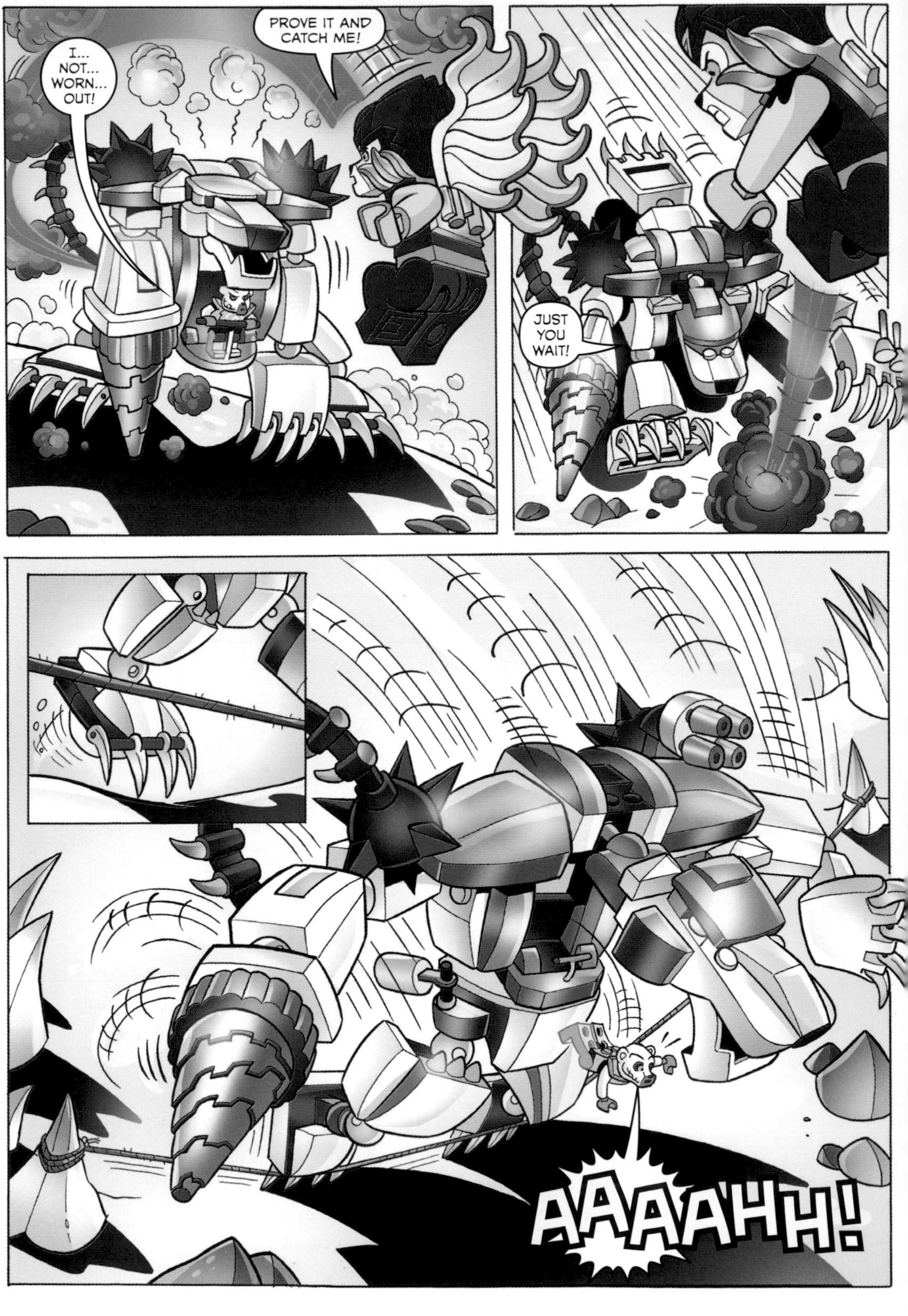
PROVE IT AND CATCH ME!
I... NOT... WORN... OUT!
JUST YOU WAIT!
AAAAHH!

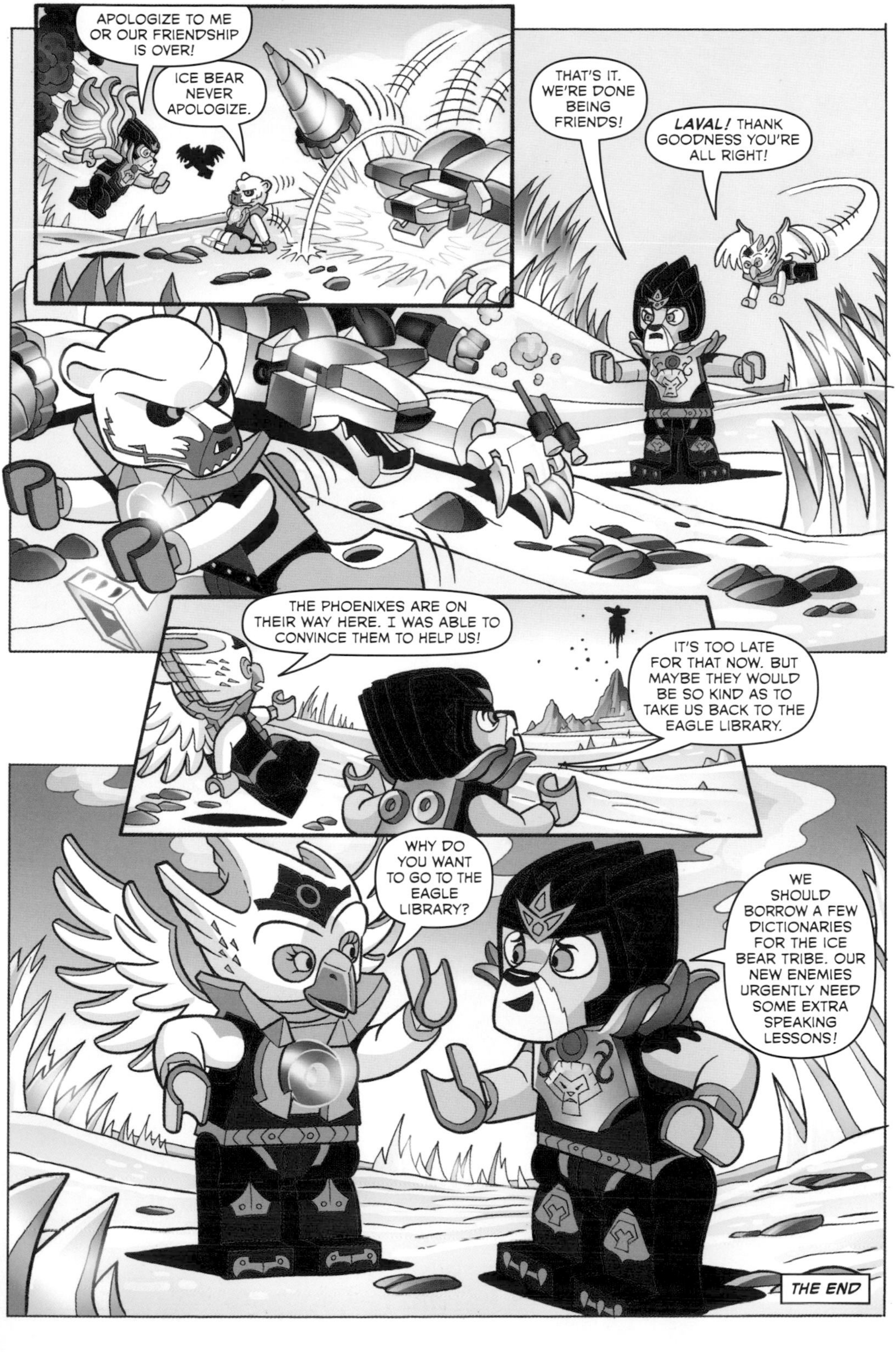
APOLOGIZE TO ME OR OUR FRIENDSHIP IS OVER!
ICE BEAR NEVER APOLOGIZE.
THAT'S IT. WE'RE DONE BEING FRIENDS!
LAVAL! THANK GOODNESS YOU'RE ALL RIGHT!
THE PHOENIXES ARE ON THEIR WAY HERE. I WAS ABLE TO CONVINCE THEM TO HELP US!
IT'S TOO LATE FOR THAT NOW. BUT MAYBE THEY WOULD BE SO KIND AS TO TAKE US BACK TO THE EAGLE LIBRARY.
WHY DO YOU WANT TO GO TO THE EAGLE LIBRARY?
WE SHOULD BORROW A FEW DICTIONARIES FOR THE ICE BEAR TRIBE. OUR NEW ENEMIES URGENTLY NEED SOME EXTRA SPEAKING LESSONS!
THE END

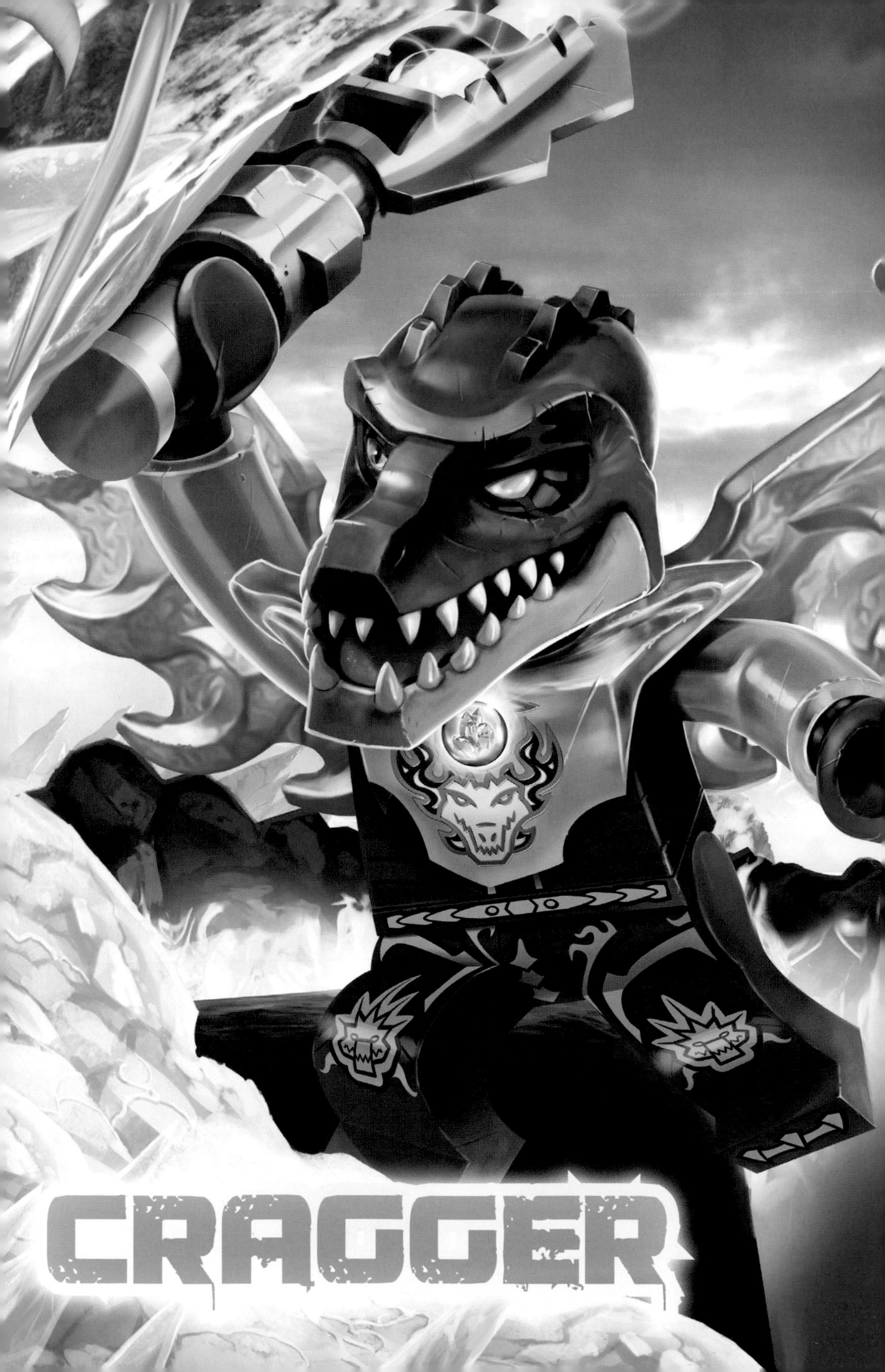
CRAGGER

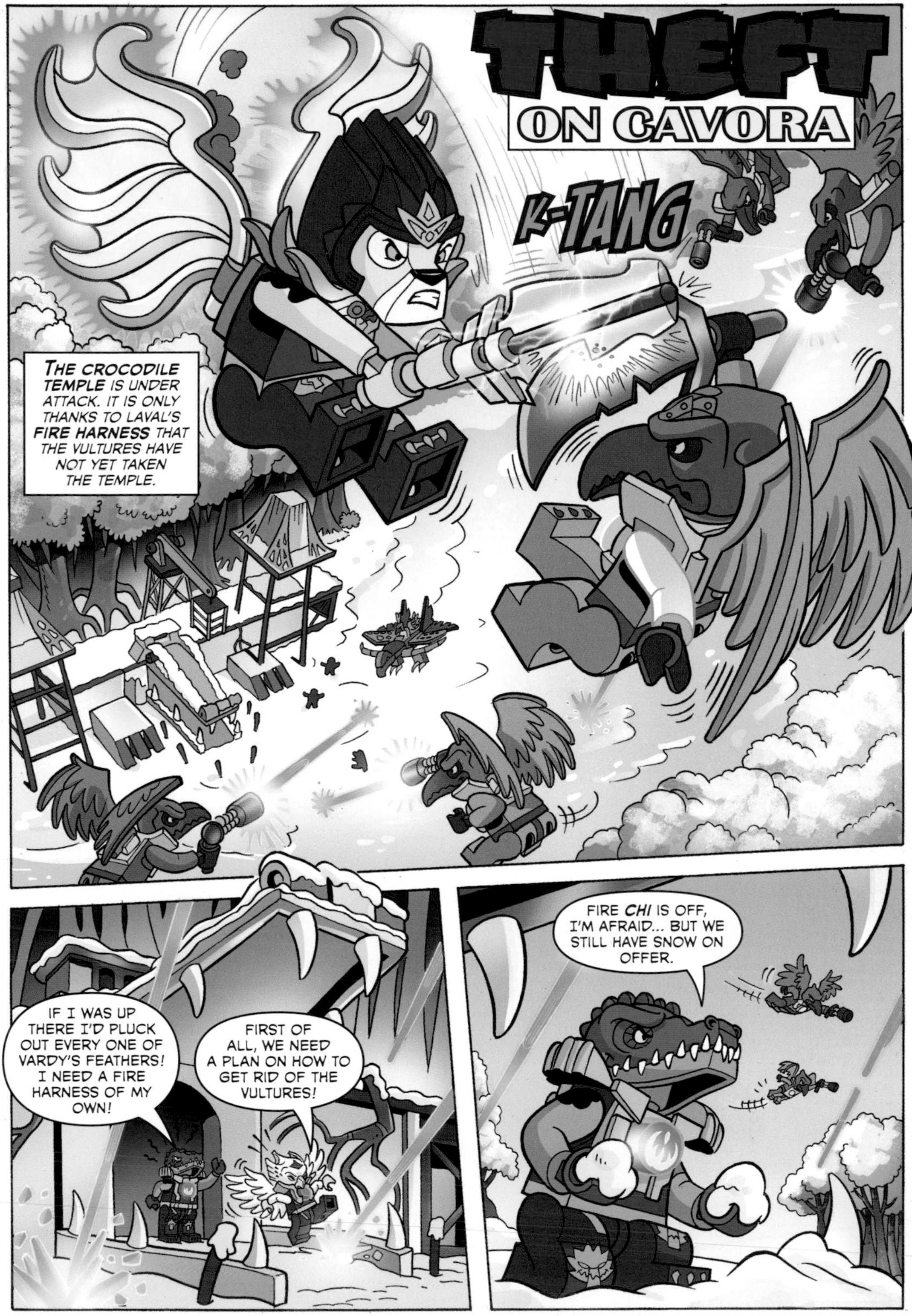
THEFT ON CAVORA
K-TANG
THE CROCODILE TEMPLE IS UNDER ATTACK. IT IS ONLY THANKS TO LAVAL'S FIRE HARNESS THAT THE VULTURES HAVE NOT YET TAKEN THE TEMPLE.
IF I WAS UP THERE I'D PLUCK OUT EVERY ONE OF VARDY'S FEATHERS! I NEED A FIRE HARNESS OF MY OWN!
FIRST OF ALL, WE NEED A PLAN ON HOW TO GET RID OF THE VULTURES!
FIRE CHI IS OFF, I'M AFRAID... BUT WE STILL HAVE SNOW ON OFFER.

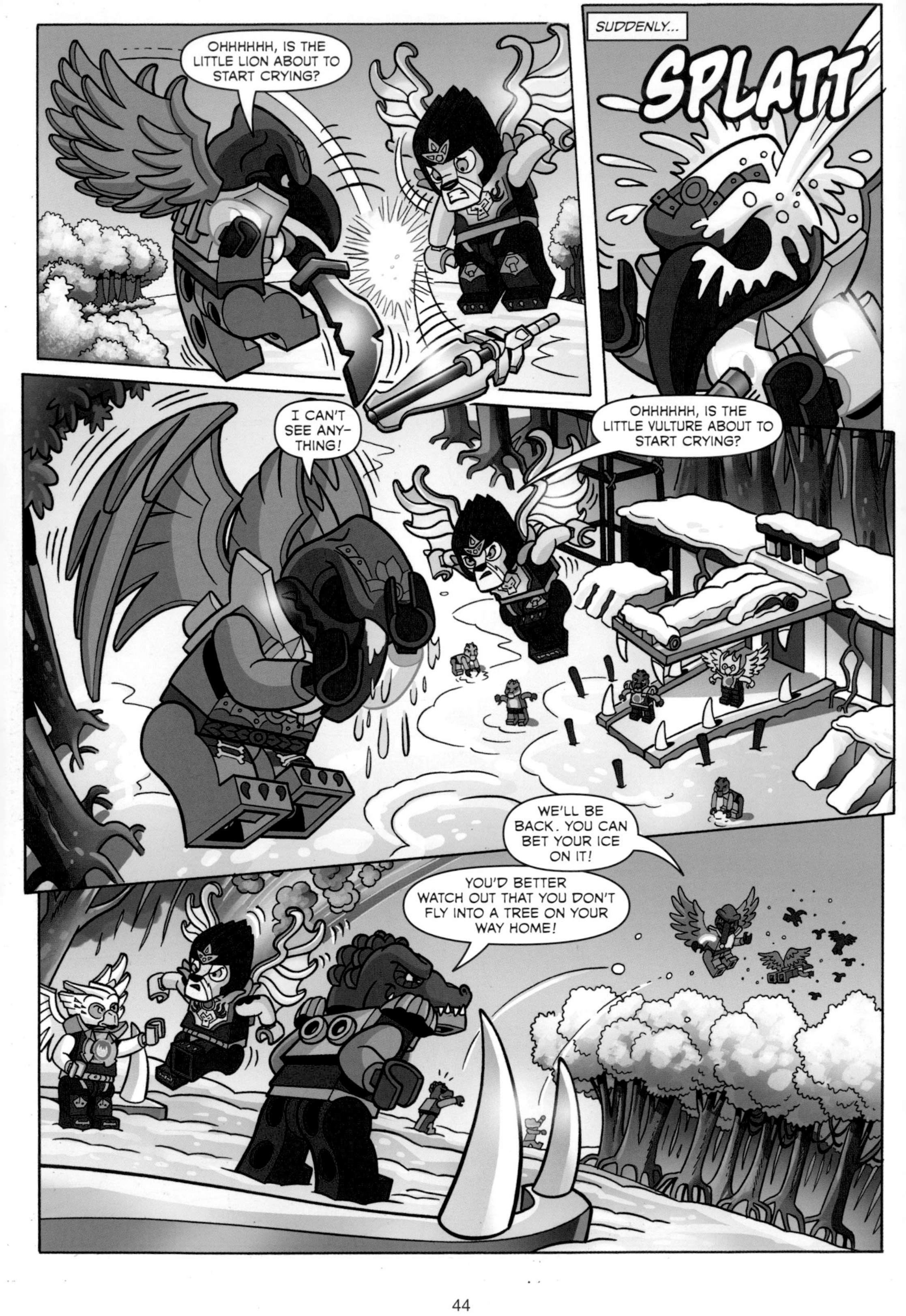
OHHHHHH, IS THE LITTLE LION ABOUT TO START CRYING?
SUDDENLY...
SPLATT
I CAN'T SEE ANY-THING!
OHHHHHH, IS THE LITTLE VULTURE ABOUT TO START CRYING?
WE'LL BE BACK. YOU CAN BET YOUR ICE ON IT!
YOU'D BETTER WATCH OUT THAT YOU DON'T FLY INTO A TREE ON YOUR WAY HOME!

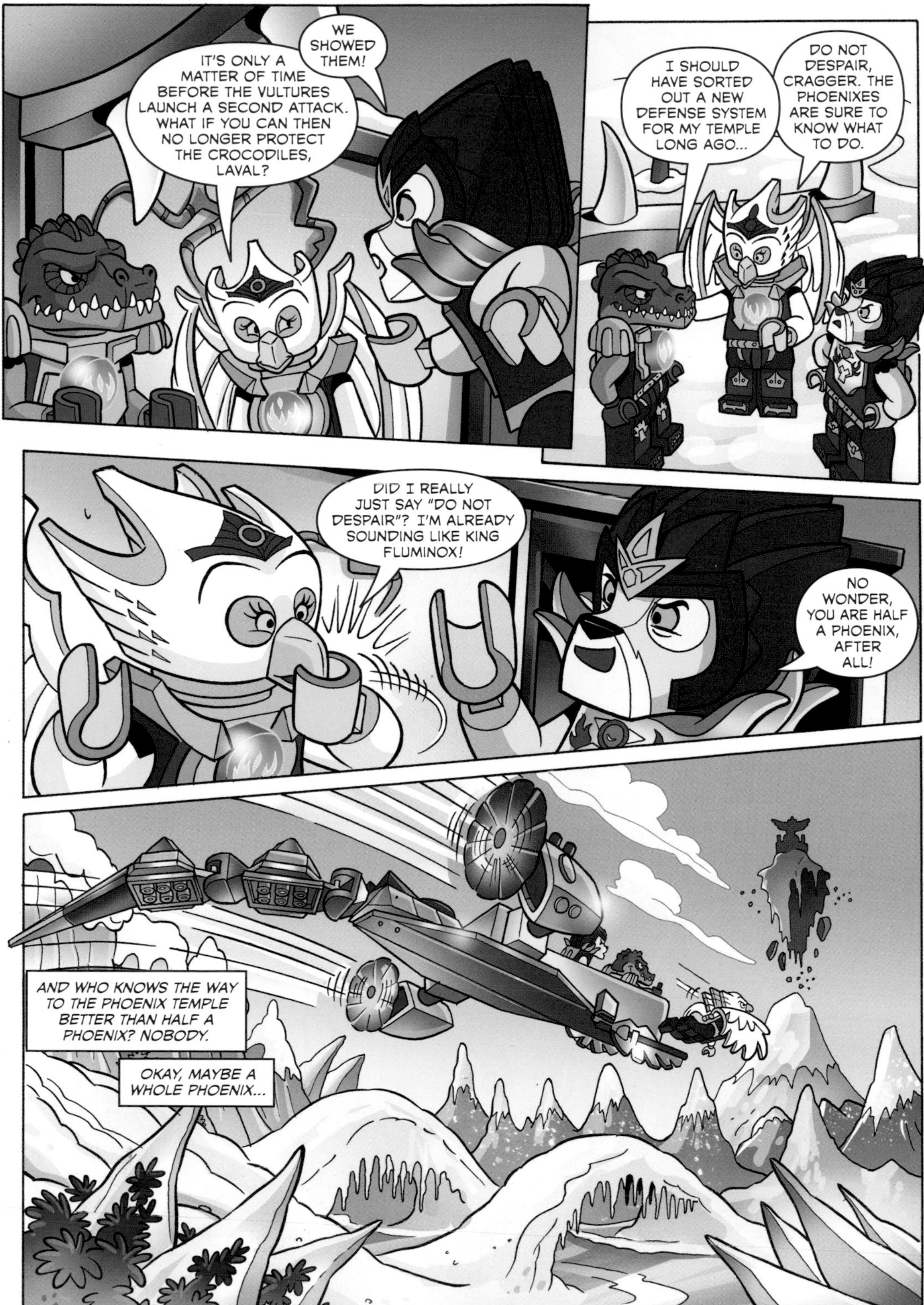
IT'S ONLY A MATTER OF TIME BEFORE THE VULTURES LAUNCH A SECOND ATTACK. WHAT IF YOU CAN THEN NO LONGER PROTECT THE CROCODILES, LAVAL?
WE SHOWED THEM!
I SHOULD HAVE SORTED OUT A NEW DEFENSE SYSTEM FOR MY TEMPLE LONG AGO...
DO NOT DESPAIR, CRAGGER. THE PHOENIXES ARE SURE TO KNOW WHAT TO DO.
DID I REALLY JUST SAY "DO NOT DESPAIR"? I'M ALREADY SOUNDING LIKE KING FLUMINOX!
NO WONDER, YOU ARE HALF A PHOENIX, AFTER ALL!
AND WHO KNOWS THE WAY TO THE PHOENIX TEMPLE BETTER THAN HALF A PHOENIX? NOBODY.
OKAY, MAYBE A WHOLE PHOENIX...

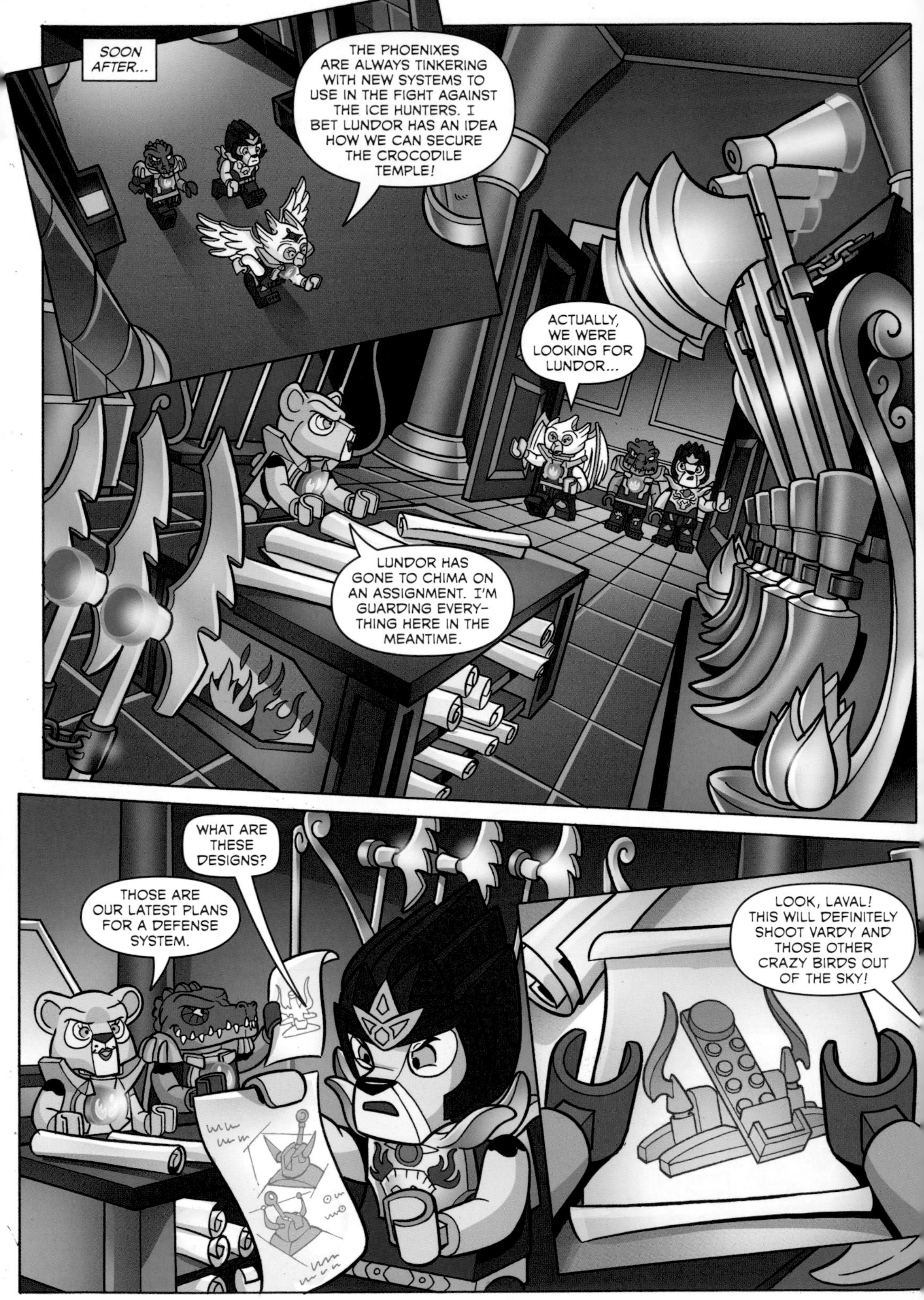
SOON AFTER...
THE PHOENIXES ARE ALWAYS TINKERING WITH NEW SYSTEMS TO USE IN THE FIGHT AGAINST THE ICE HUNTERS. I BET LUNDOR HAS AN IDEA HOW WE CAN SECURE THE CROCODILE TEMPLE!
ACTUALLY, WE WERE LOOKING FOR LUNDOR...
LUNDOR HAS GONE TO CHIMA ON AN ASSIGNMENT. I'M GUARDING EVERY-THING HERE IN THE MEANTIME.
WHAT ARE THESE DESIGNS?
THOSE ARE OUR LATEST PLANS FOR A DEFENSE SYSTEM.
LOOK, LAVAL! THIS WILL DEFINITELY SHOOT VARDY AND THOSE OTHER CRAZY BIRDS OUT OF THE SKY!

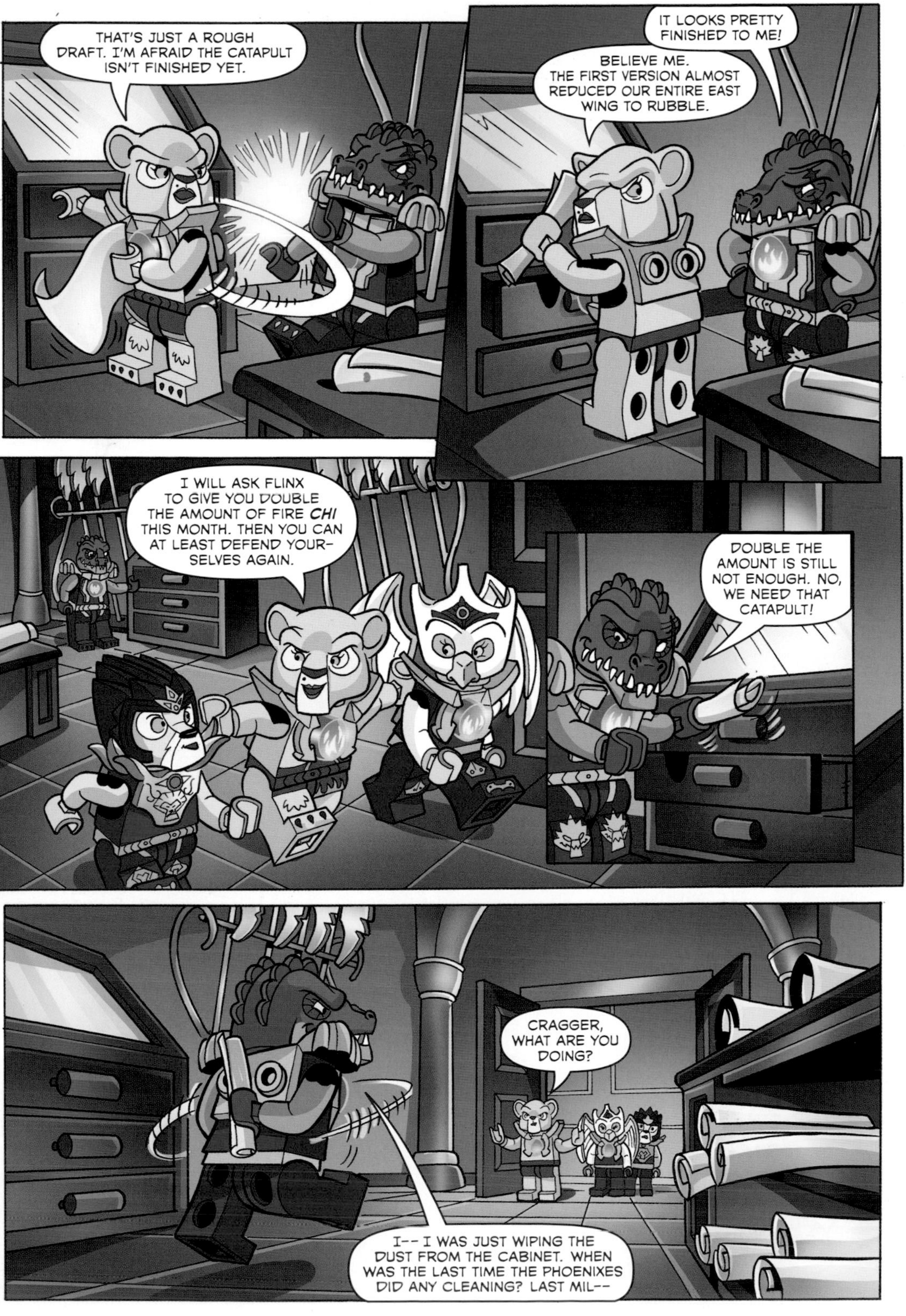
THAT'S JUST A ROUGH DRAFT. I'M AFRAID THE CATAPULT ISN'T FINISHED YET.
IT LOOKS PRETTY FINISHED TO ME!
BELIEVE ME. THE FIRST VERSION ALMOST REDUCED OUR ENTIRE EAST WING TO RUBBLE.
I WILL ASK FLINX TO GIVE YOU DOUBLE THE AMOUNT OF FIRE *CHI* THIS MONTH. THEN YOU CAN AT LEAST DEFEND YOURSELVES AGAIN.
DOUBLE THE AMOUNT IS STILL NOT ENOUGH. NO, WE NEED THAT CATAPULT!
CRAGGER, WHAT ARE YOU DOING?
I-- I WAS JUST WIPING THE DUST FROM THE CABINET. WHEN WAS THE LAST TIME THE PHOENIXES DID ANY CLEANING? LAST MIL--

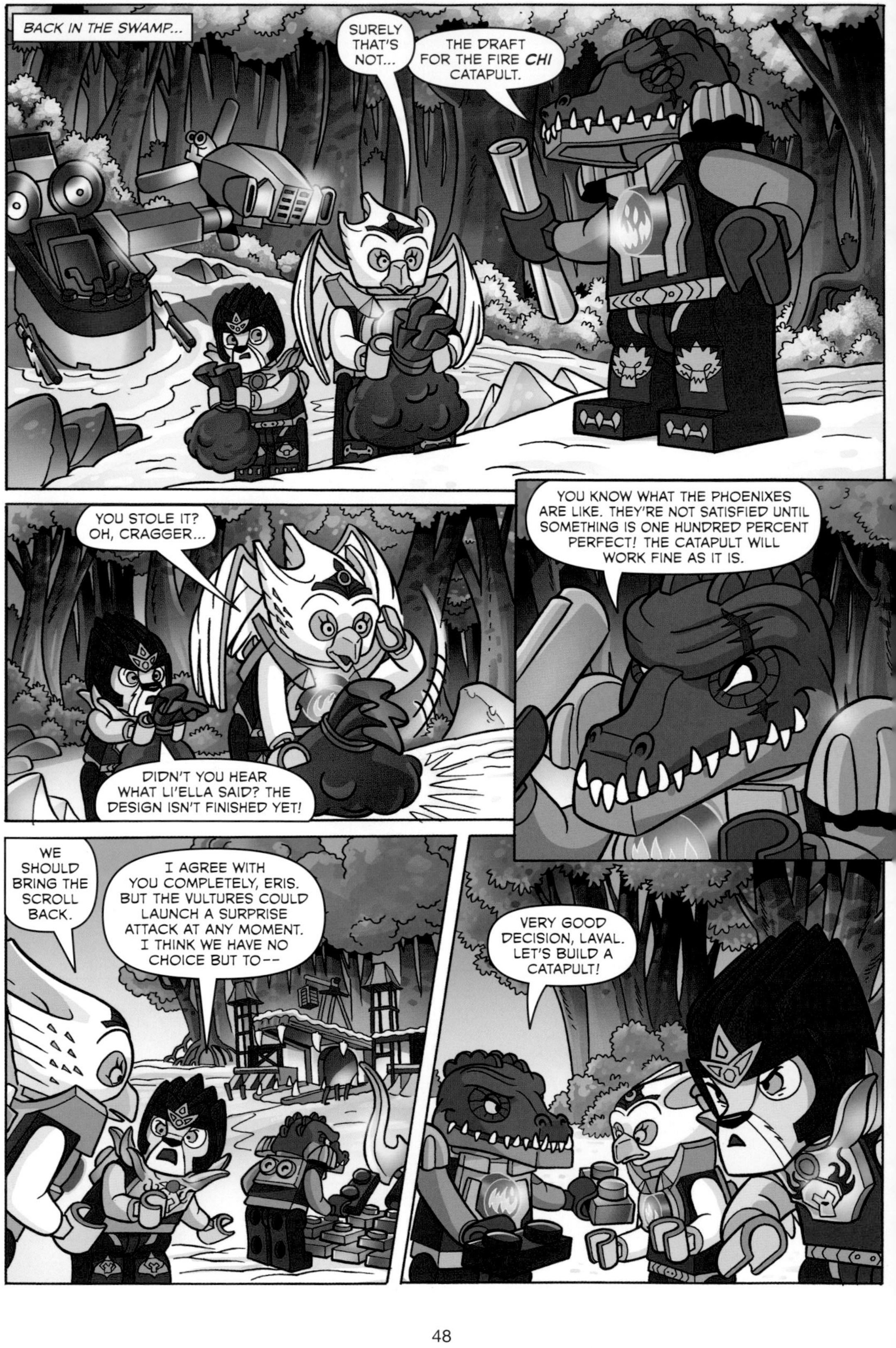
BACK IN THE SWAMP...
SURELY THAT'S NOT...
THE DRAFT FOR THE FIRE *CHI* CATAPULT.
YOU STOLE IT? OH, CRAGGER...
DIDN'T YOU HEAR WHAT LI'ELLA SAID? THE DESIGN ISN'T FINISHED YET!
YOU KNOW WHAT THE PHOENIXES ARE LIKE. THEY'RE NOT SATISFIED UNTIL SOMETHING IS ONE HUNDRED PERCENT PERFECT! THE CATAPULT WILL WORK FINE AS IT IS.
WE SHOULD BRING THE SCROLL BACK.
I AGREE WITH YOU COMPLETELY, ERIS. BUT THE VULTURES COULD LAUNCH A SURPRISE ATTACK AT ANY MOMENT. I THINK WE HAVE NO CHOICE BUT TO--
VERY GOOD DECISION, LAVAL. LET'S BUILD A CATAPULT!

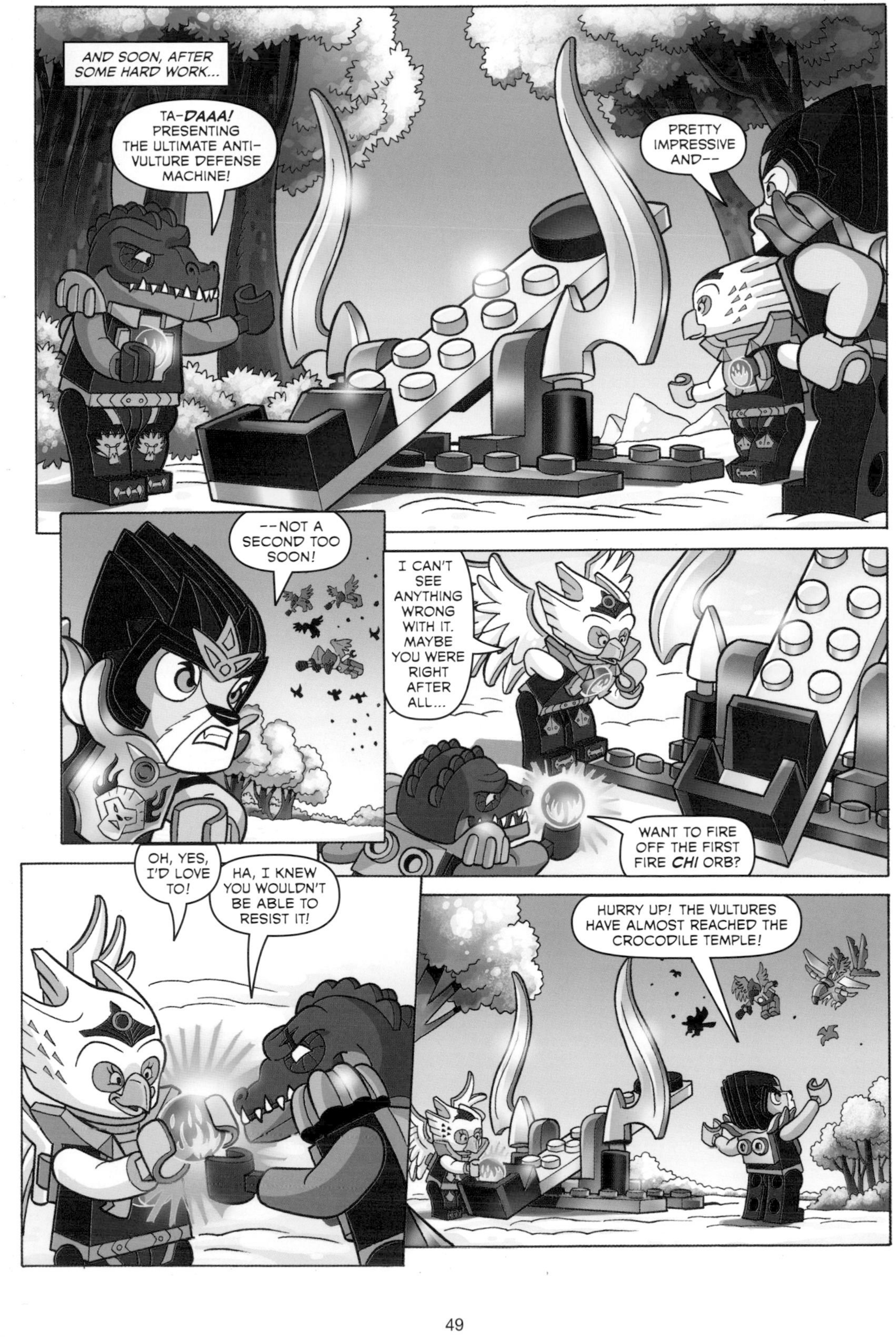
AND SOON, AFTER SOME HARD WORK...
TA-DAAA! PRESENTING THE ULTIMATE ANTI-VULTURE DEFENSE MACHINE!
PRETTY IMPRESSIVE AND--
--NOT A SECOND TOO SOON!
I CAN'T SEE ANYTHING WRONG WITH IT. MAYBE YOU WERE RIGHT AFTER ALL...
WANT TO FIRE OFF THE FIRST FIRE CHI ORB?
OH, YES, I'D LOVE TO!
HA, I KNEW YOU WOULDN'T BE ABLE TO RESIST IT!
HURRY UP! THE VULTURES HAVE ALMOST REACHED THE CROCODILE TEMPLE!

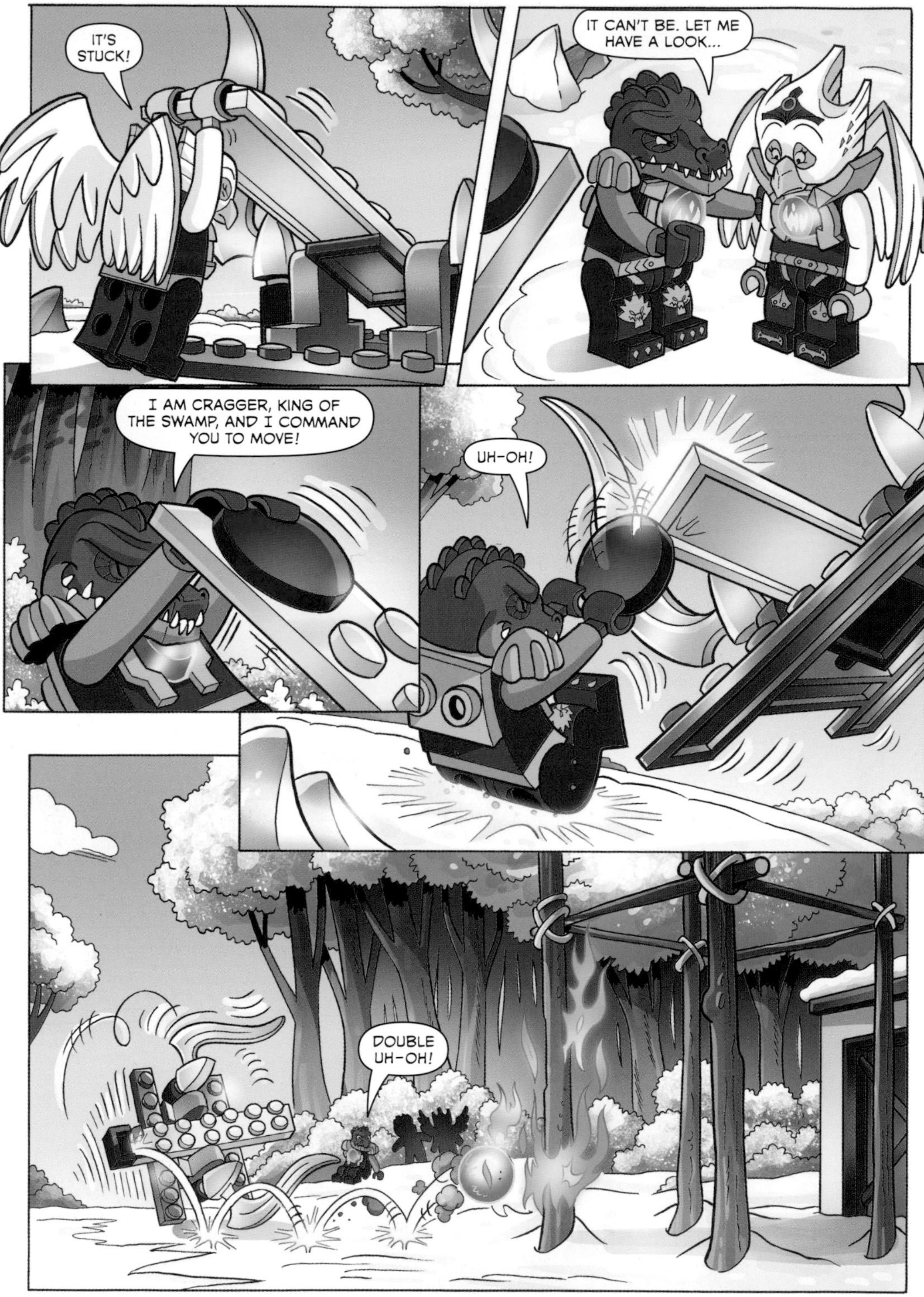
IT'S STUCK!
IT CAN'T BE. LET ME HAVE A LOOK...
I AM CRAGGER, KING OF THE SWAMP, AND I COMMAND YOU TO MOVE!
UH-OH!
DOUBLE UH-OH!

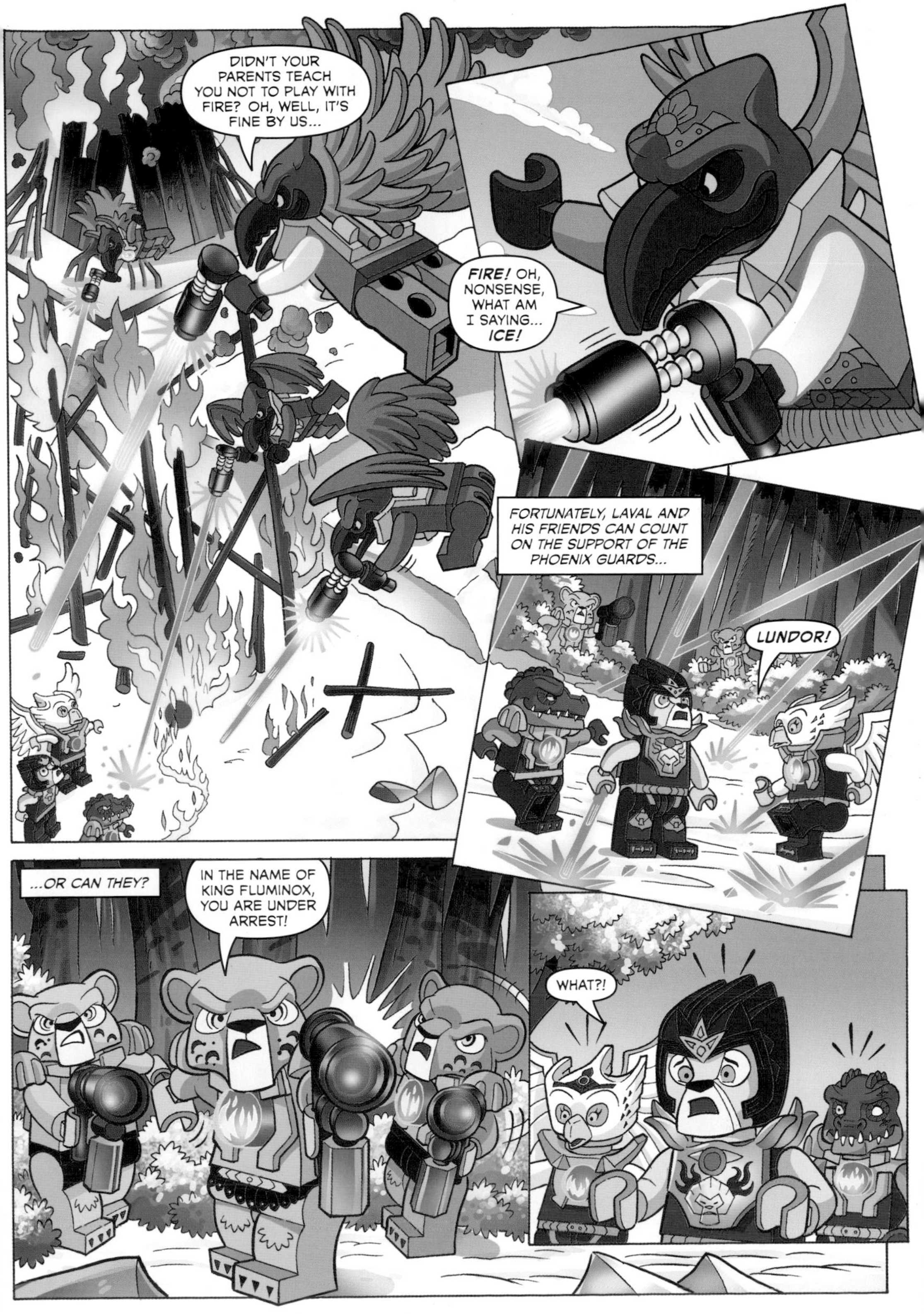
DIDN'T YOUR PARENTS TEACH YOU NOT TO PLAY WITH FIRE? OH, WELL, IT'S FINE BY US...
FIRE! OH, NONSENSE, WHAT AM I SAYING... ICE!
FORTUNATELY, LAVAL AND HIS FRIENDS CAN COUNT ON THE SUPPORT OF THE PHOENIX GUARDS...
LUNDOR!
...OR CAN THEY?
IN THE NAME OF KING FLUMINOX, YOU ARE UNDER ARREST!
WHAT?!

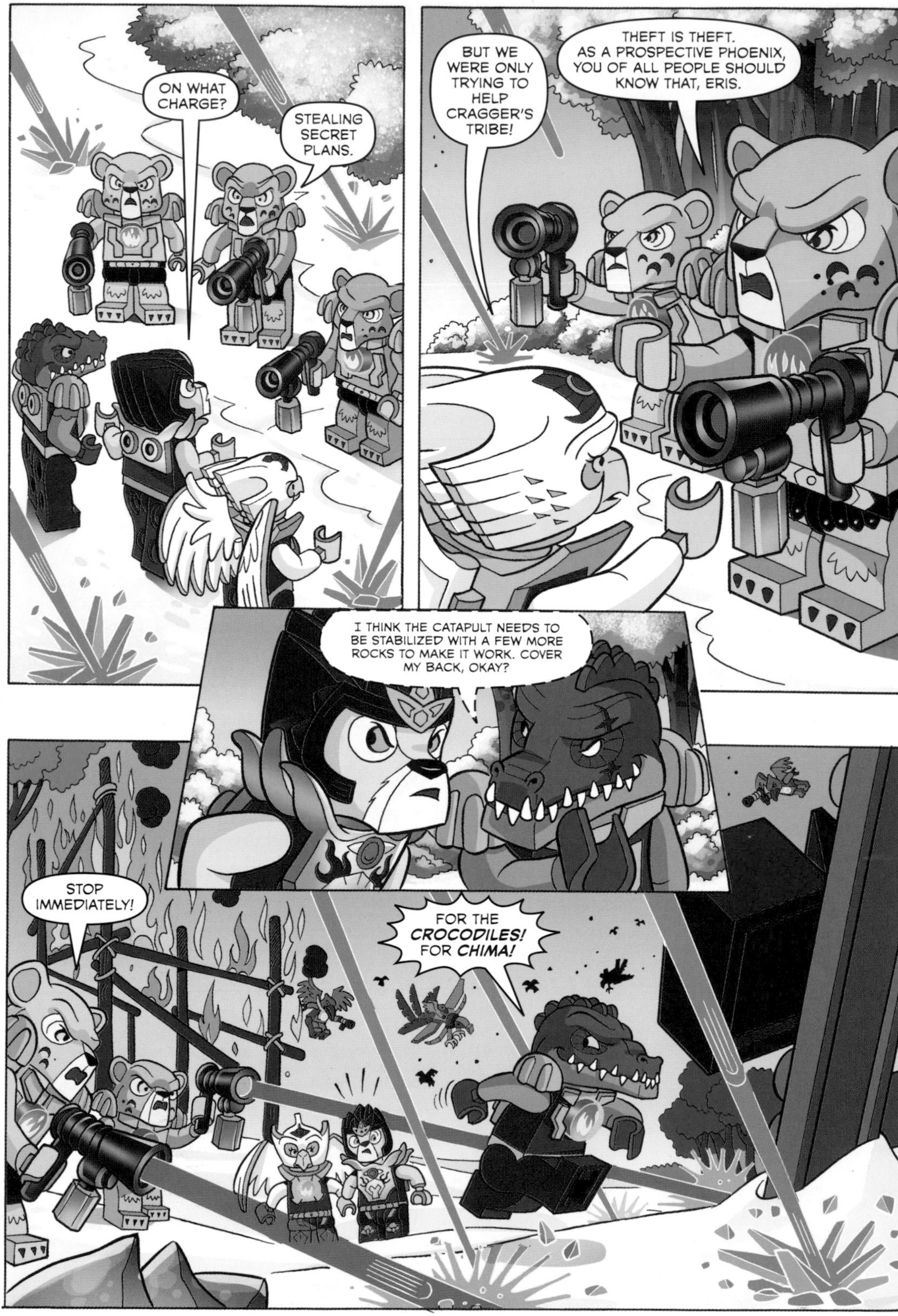

ON WHAT CHARGE?
STEALING SECRET PLANS.
BUT WE WERE ONLY TRYING TO HELP CRAGGER'S TRIBE!
THEFT IS THEFT. AS A PROSPECTIVE PHOENIX, YOU OF ALL PEOPLE SHOULD KNOW THAT, ERIS.
I THINK THE CATAPULT NEEDS TO BE STABILIZED WITH A FEW MORE ROCKS TO MAKE IT WORK. COVER MY BACK, OKAY?
STOP IMMEDIATELY!
FOR THE *CROCODILES!* FOR *CHIMA!*

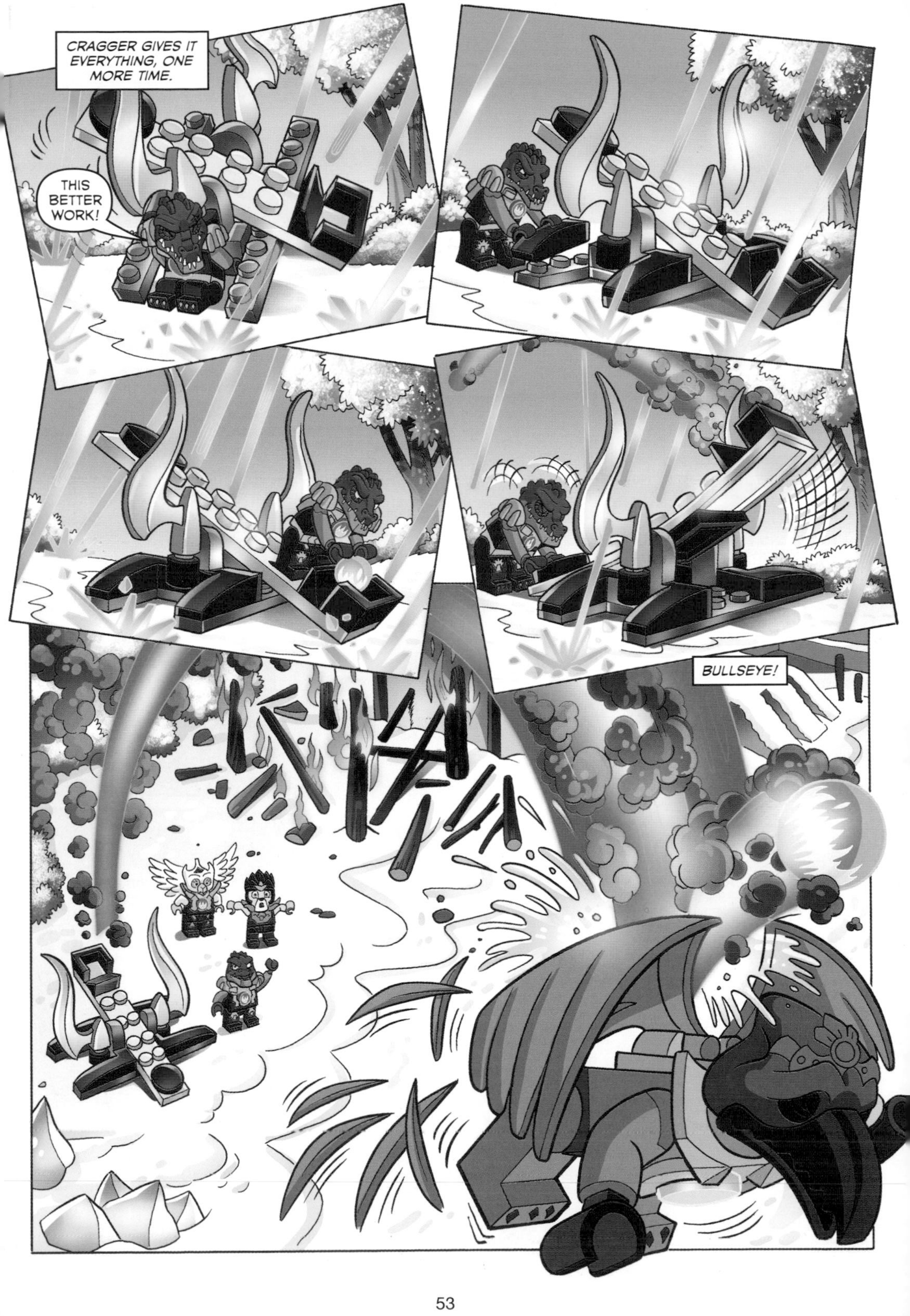

CRAGGER GIVES IT EVERYTHING, ONE MORE TIME.
THIS BETTER WORK!
BULLSEYE!

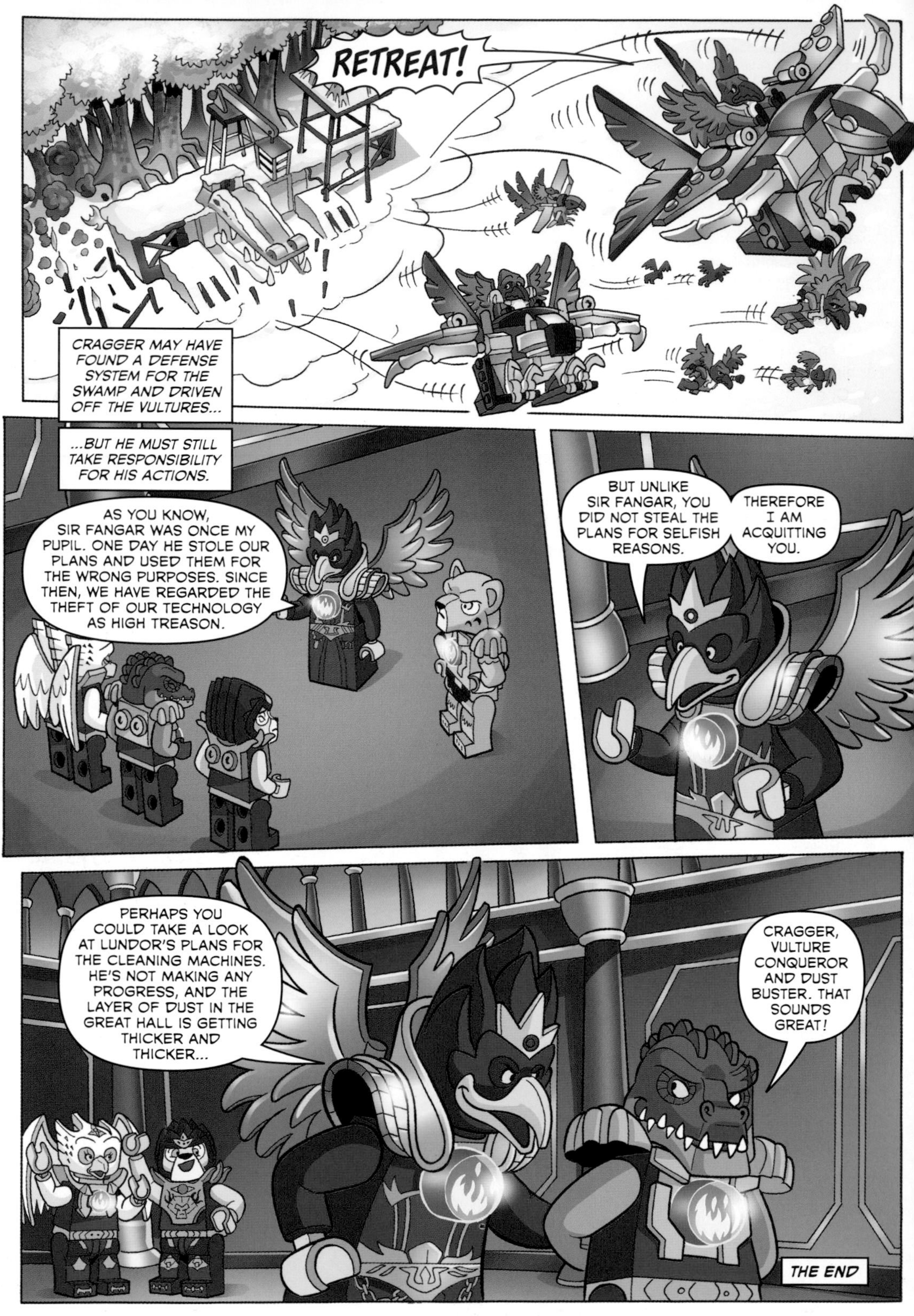
RETREAT!
CRAGGER MAY HAVE FOUND A DEFENSE SYSTEM FOR THE SWAMP AND DRIVEN OFF THE VULTURES...
...BUT HE MUST STILL TAKE RESPONSIBILITY FOR HIS ACTIONS.
AS YOU KNOW, SIR FANGAR WAS ONCE MY PUPIL. ONE DAY HE STOLE OUR PLANS AND USED THEM FOR THE WRONG PURPOSES. SINCE THEN, WE HAVE REGARDED THE THEFT OF OUR TECHNOLOGY AS HIGH TREASON.
BUT UNLIKE SIR FANGAR, YOU DID NOT STEAL THE PLANS FOR SELFISH REASONS.
THEREFORE I AM ACQUITTING YOU.
PERHAPS YOU COULD TAKE A LOOK AT LUNDOR'S PLANS FOR THE CLEANING MACHINES. HE'S NOT MAKING ANY PROGRESS, AND THE LAYER OF DUST IN THE GREAT HALL IS GETTING THICKER AND THICKER...
CRAGGER, VULTURE CONQUEROR AND DUST BUSTER. THAT SOUNDS GREAT!
THE END

WATCH OUT FOR PAPERCUTZ™

Welcome to the unexpected frosty fifth LEGO ® LEGENDS OF CHIMA graphic novel, by Yannick Grotholt and Comicon, from Papercutz—those never-say-die folks dedicated to publishing great graphic novels for all ages. I'm Jim Salicrup, the somewhat embarrassed Editor-in-Chief and honorary member of the Beavers! I'm here to explain why there's a fifth volume of LEGO LEGENDS OF CHIMA, when I said in Vol. 4 that *that* was the last CHIMA graphic novel...

Unlike the LEGO NINJAGO graphic novels, which were produced by Papercutz, working with writer Greg Farshtey and artists PH Henrique and Jolyon Yates, the LEGO LEGENDS OF CHIMA graphic novels are produced by German publisher Blue Ocean, working with writer Yannick Grotholt and artists Comicon. They've published a translated version of the NINJAGO comics we've created over in Germany, and we've been publishing CHIMA in North America. Our license to publish LEGO LEGENDS OF CHIMA was reaching its end, and when it appeared that we had published everything that Blue Ocean had created, we decide to end LEGO LEGENDS OF CHIMA with #4. But it seems something must've got lost in translation, and lo and behold! There were stories that we hadn't yet published. Enough stories, in fact, for two more LEGO LEGENDS OF CHIMA graphic novels—of which, this is the first one!

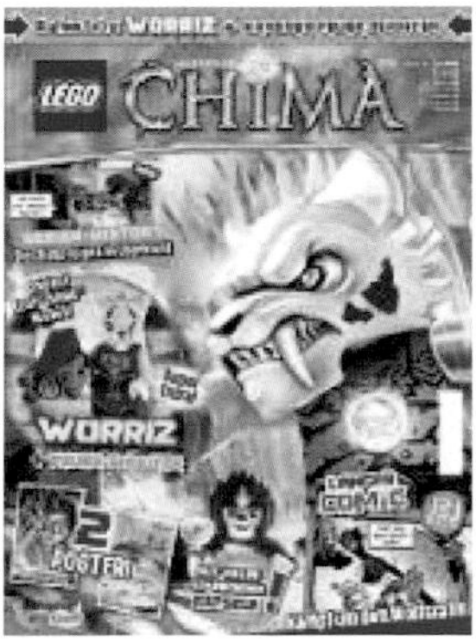
LEGO CHIMA
WORRIZ

So, we're back! And not just for this volume, but there will also be one more volume of LEGO LEGENDS OF CHIMA as well! We're thrilled we were able to straighten everything out, and thank our friends at Blue Ocean for their patience and for helping us figure this all out.

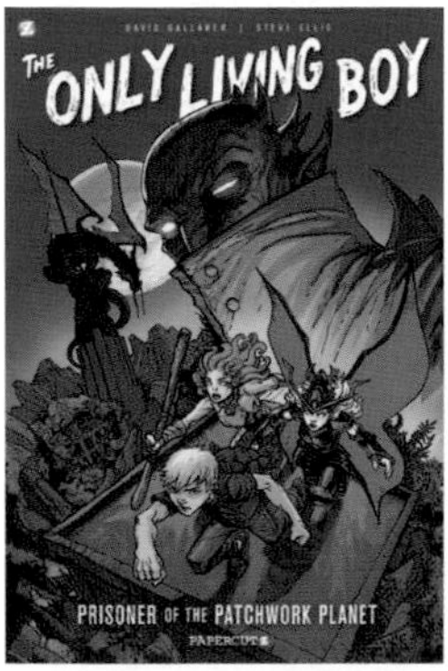
DAVID GALLAHER | STEVE ELLIS
THE ONLY LIVING BOY
PRISONER OF THE PATCHWORK PLANET
PAPERCUTZ

In the meantime, we've been busier than ever at Papercutz. As usual, you can go to Papercutz.com to see all of the exciting new projects that we have planned for you. Perhaps the most action-packed is ONLY LIVING BOY. It's a graphic novel series collecting the comics that were originally published online by writer David Gallaher and artist Steve Ellis. It's about young Erik Farrell, who is lost, without his memory, in an unfamiliar world, where he must piece together a new life for himself. Can he survive as the only living boy left in the world?

There's also a new series coming from legendary comics creator (and a true hero of mine) Stan Lee! Based on his hit new YA series called THE ZODIAC LEGACY, writer Stuart Moore and artist Paris Cullins create new stories the fit perfectly into the book series. The story begins when twelve magical superpowers are unleashed on the world, and a Chinese-American teenager named Steven Lee is thrown into the middle of an epic global chase. He'll have to master strange powers, outrun super-powered mercenaries, and unlock the secret to the mysterious powers of the Zodiac.

There's plenty more—such as an all-new NICKELODEON MAGAZINE, DISNEY GRAPHIC NOVELS, and DENNIS THE MENACE—but before we forget, let me remind you that there still is one more LEGO LEGENDS OF CHIMA graphic novel coming your way from Papercutz! Don't miss LEGO LEGENDS OF CHIMA #6 "Playing with Fire!" coming soon!

Thanks,

Jim

STAY IN TOUCH!

EMAIL:	salicrup@papercutz.com
WEB:	papercutz.com
TWITTER:	@papercutzgn
FACEBOOK:	PAPERCUTZGRAPHICNOVELS
FAN MAIL:	Papercutz, 160 Broadway, Suite 700, East Wing, New York, NY 10038

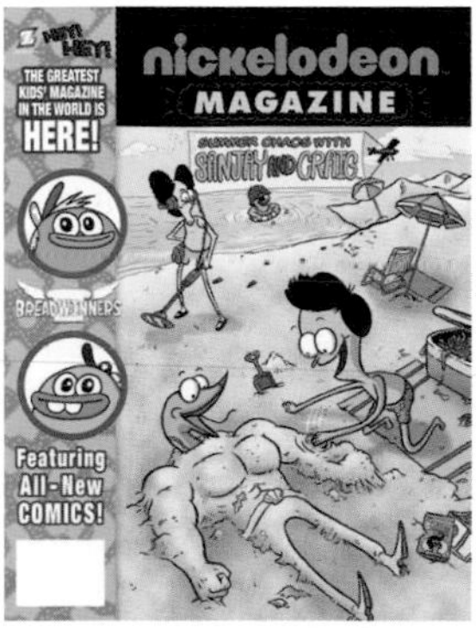
THE GREATEST KIDS' MAGAZINE IN THE WORLD IS HERE!
nickelodeon
MAGAZINE
Featuring All-New COMICS!

LEGO® GRAPHIC NOVELS AVAILABLE FROM PAPERCUTZ™

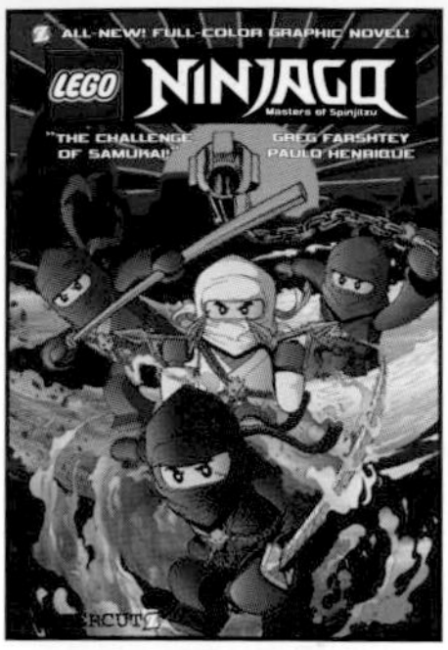
ALL-NEW! FULL-COLOR GRAPHIC NOVEL!
LEGO NINJAGO
"THE CHALLENGE OF SAMURAI"
GREG FARSHTEY
PAULO HENRIQUE
LEGO NINJAGO #1

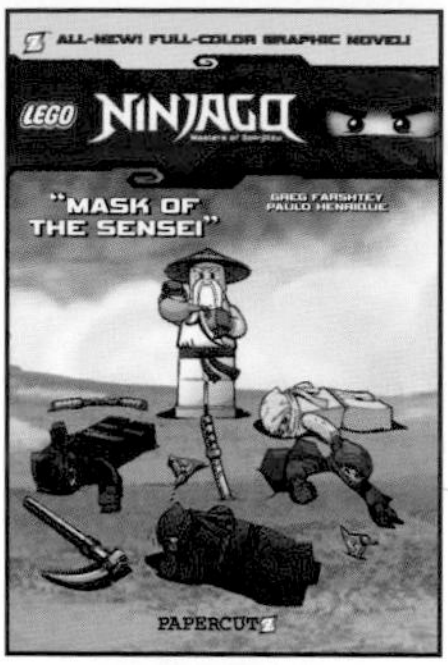
ALL-NEW! FULL-COLOR GRAPHIC NOVEL!
LEGO NINJAGO
"MASK OF THE SENSEI"
PAPERCUTZ
LEGO NINJAGO #2

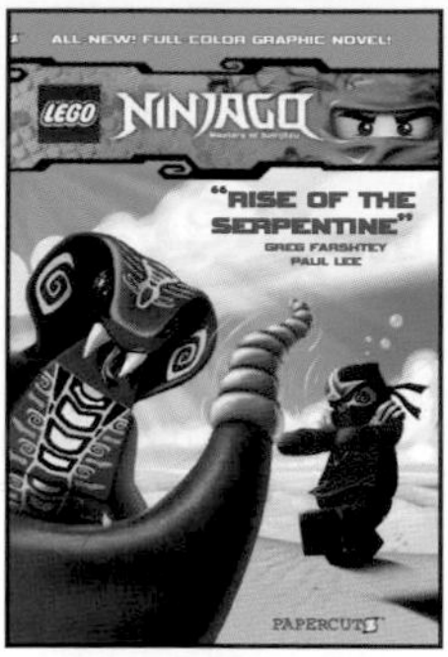
ALL-NEW! FULL-COLOR GRAPHIC NOVEL!
LEGO NINJAGO
"RISE OF THE SERPENTINE"
GREG FARSHTEY
PAUL LEE
PAPERCUTZ
LEGO NINJAGO #3

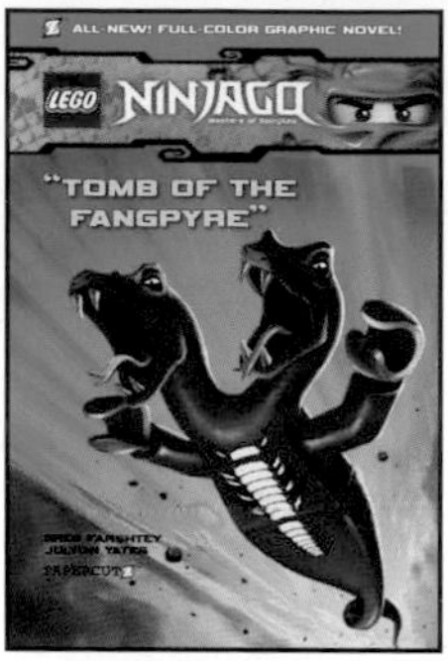
ALL-NEW! FULL-COLOR GRAPHIC NOVEL!
LEGO NINJAGO
"TOMB OF THE FANGPYRE"
LEGO NINJAGO #4

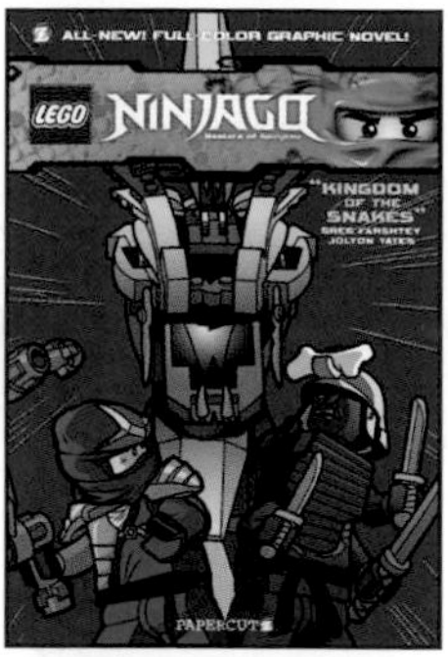
ALL-NEW! FULL-COLOR GRAPHIC NOVEL!
LEGO NINJAGO
"KINGDOM OF THE SNAKES"
PAPERCUTZ
LEGO NINJAGO #5

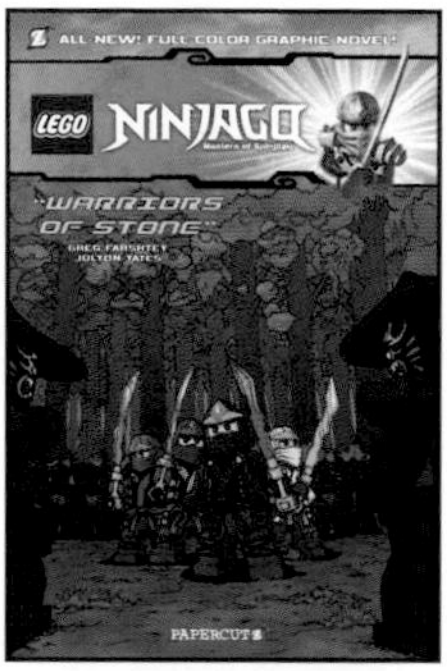
ALL-NEW! FULL-COLOR GRAPHIC NOVEL!
LEGO NINJAGO
"WARRIORS OF STONE"
PAPERCUTZ
LEGO NINJAGO #6

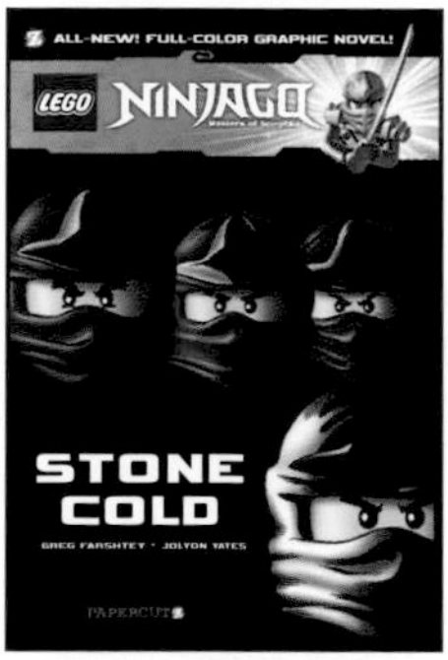
ALL-NEW! FULL-COLOR GRAPHIC NOVEL!
LEGO NINJAGO
STONE COLD
PAPERCUTZ
LEGO NINJAGO #7

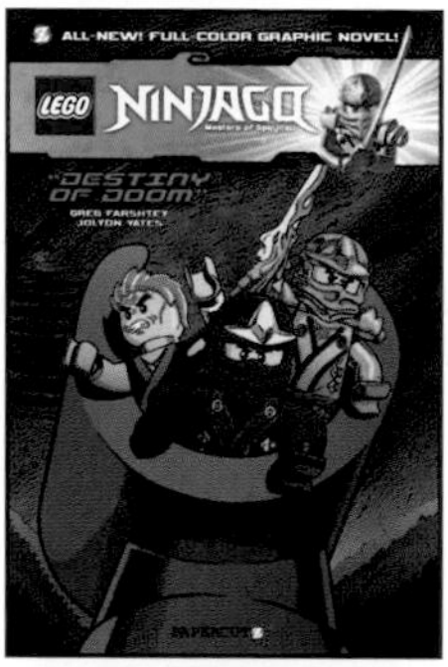
ALL-NEW! FULL-COLOR GRAPHIC NOVEL!
LEGO NINJAGO
"DESTINY OF DOOM"
LEGO NINJAGO #8

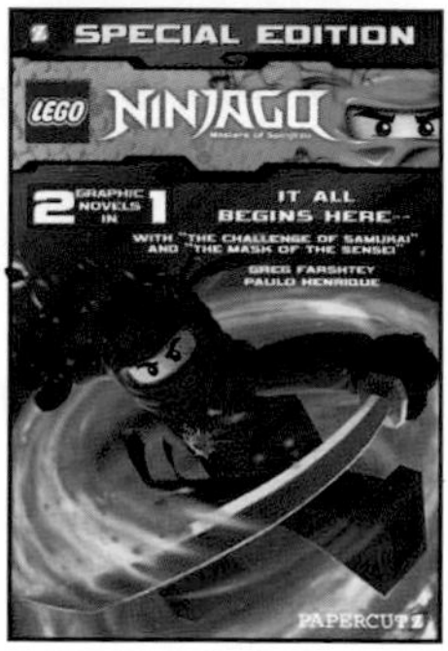
SPECIAL EDITION
LEGO NINJAGO
2 GRAPHIC NOVELS IN 1
IT ALL BEGINS HERE--
WITH "THE CHALLENGE OF SAMURAI" AND "THE MASK OF THE SENSEI"
PAPERCUTZ
SPECIAL EDITION #1
(Features stories from LEGO NINJAGO #1 & #2.)

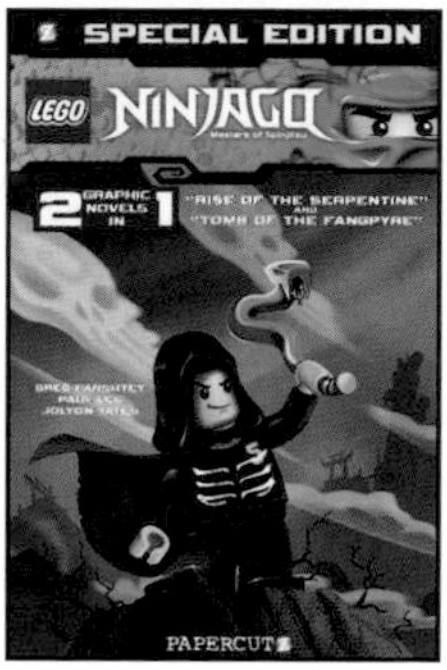
SPECIAL EDITION
LEGO NINJAGO
2 GRAPHIC NOVELS IN 1
"RISE OF THE SERPENTINE" AND "TOMB OF THE FANGPYRE"
PAPERCUTZ
SPECIAL EDITION #2
(Features stories from LEGO NINJAGO #3 & #4.)

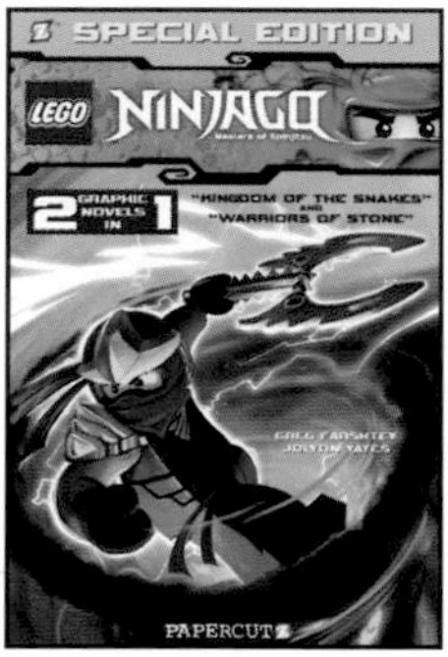
SPECIAL EDITION
LEGO NINJAGO
2 GRAPHIC NOVELS IN 1
"KINGDOM OF THE SNAKES" AND "WARRIORS OF STONE"
PAPERCUTZ
SPECIAL EDITION #3
(Features stories from LEGO NINJAGO #5 & #6.)

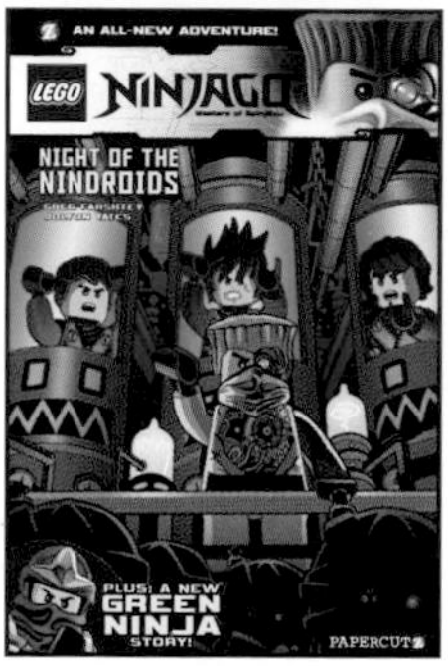
AN ALL-NEW ADVENTURE!
LEGO NINJAGO
NIGHT OF THE NINDROIDS
PLUS: A NEW GREEN NINJA STORY!
PAPERCUTZ
LEGO NINJAGO #9

LEGO® NINJAGO graphic novels are available in paperback and hardcover at booksellers everywhere.

LEGO® NINJAGO #1-11 are $6.99 in paperback, and $10.99 in hardcover. LEGO NINJAGO SPECIAL EDITION #1-3 are $10.99 in paperback only. You can also order online at papercutz.com. Or call 1-800-886-1223, Monday through Friday, 9 – 5 EST. MC, Visa, and AmEx accepted. To order by mail, please add $4.00 for postage and handling for first book ordered, $1.00 for each additional book and make check payable to NBM Publishing. Send to: Papercutz, 160 Broadway, Suite 700, East Wing, New York, NY 10038.

LEGO NINJAGO graphic novels are also available digitally wherever e-books are sold.

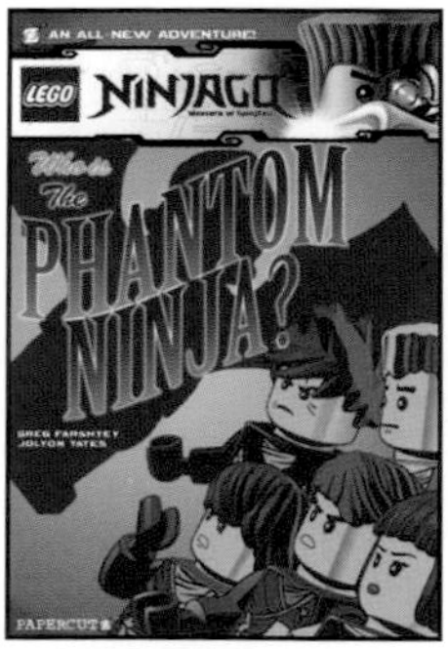
AN ALL-NEW ADVENTURE!
LEGO NINJAGO
Who is The PHANTOM NINJA?
PAPERCUTZ
LEGO NINJAGO #10

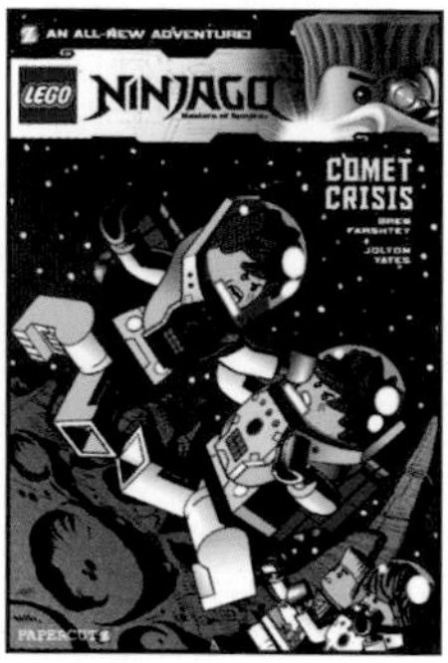
AN ALL-NEW ADVENTURE!
LEGO NINJAGO
COMET CRISIS
PAPERCUTZ
LEGO NINJAGO #11